# LEXIE'S UNFORESEEN BENEFACTOR

Twenty-year-old Lexie fears their family-run hotel may be heading for bankruptcy due to her mismanagement. She doesn't know which way to turn when, out of the blue, her father and his stepson Jake get in touch. Lexie had always thought her father was dead, and is startled by his sudden appearance, while Jake proves to be more than a little intimidating. When he offers a way out of her financial problems, Lexie reluctantly accepts, only to discover how authoritarian he can be . . .

Pl

Dych

EILEEN KNOWLES

# LEXIE'S UNFORESEEN BENEFACTOR

*Complete and Unabridged*

## LINFORD
*Leicester*

First published in Great Britain in 2004

First Linford Edition
published 2019

*A catalogue record for this book is available
from the British Library.*

ISBN 978–1–4448–3969–2

# 1

Lexie knew precisely how the poor little sparrow felt as it desperately beat against the window pane trying to find a way out of her room. It should have forewarned her of the difficult day ahead, but not being particularly superstitious, Lexie simply threw open the window and helped the struggling creature escape.

How she wished she could escape so readily. Not that she wanted to leave Bay View, but she needed to find some way out of the dilemma preoccupying her every waking moment. *I suppose today I shall have to own up to my appalling blunder*, she reflected miserably. Why couldn't the bank manager see her point of view? Why indeed had there to be a change at the local branch at that critical moment?

With a huge sigh, Lexie smoothed

down her skirt, and with a last look in the mirror went down to face another day's work. Looking after the residents of the Bay View Hotel was a full-time occupation with little time to dwell on what the future might hold. The full impact of what had transpired took time to register, but it looked as if they were going to have to sell up, all because of her stupidity.

A little while later, she entered their own private sitting room sifting warily through the morning post. 'There's one for you, Mother, with a South African postmark. Got yourself a secret admirer now, have you?' With an impish smile, she handed over the pale blue airmail letter. 'Definitely a man's handwriting, I can tell.'

'Many a true word spoken in jest,' her mother replied, reaching for her spectacles. 'I expect it's someone enquiring about a booking, although the tarot cards did foresee a figure from the past arriving in the near future.'

Lexie wished her mother would

spend a little more of her time in the present and less with séances and fortune telling. 'It's marked private and confidential,' she added, going over to the writing bureau to deal with the rest of the mail, 'so it doesn't seem likely.' As she sat down, she overheard her mother give a gasp of surprise.

'Interesting after all?' she murmured, preoccupied with her own thoughts. Slitting open the envelopes, she quickly scanned the contents, relieved to note there were no bills amongst them. The only letter of concern was the one she'd been expecting from the newly appointed bank manager confirming the cancellation of their overdraft facility. He wouldn't listen when she'd explained theirs was one of the few remaining hotels in the town, and it was only a question of time before it became profitable again. She had stressed her faith in a viable future since their hotel was in such a prime position on Ravenstone's seafront, but he was unconvinced. Having heard he was young, Lexie expected him to appreciate how difficult it was for a twenty-year-old to cope in the present financial climate, but only the lack of funds in the account interested him.

'Goodness gracious,' exclaimed her mother, looking up with a startled expression. 'I don't believe it. I . . . '

'Are you all right, Mum?' Lexie bent to retrieve the envelope that had fallen from her mother's trembling fingers. 'You look like you've seen a ghost.'

Her mother nodded, smiling wanly and waving the air letter. 'It's just . . . it's so incredible . . . '

The bell at reception rang noisily, interrupting her. 'I'll go,' Lexie said, hastily pushing the morning post into the desk drawer so her mother wouldn't see it. It was September — the end of the summer season; and apart from the few permanent residents, Bay View Hotel was quiet. Ravenstone was again the sleepy seaside resort battening down for the coming winter months. Lexie knew there was little hope of raising all the money they needed easily, but she didn't wish to upset her mother with the problem just yet. She hadn't explored every possibility. Bay View was their home — where she had always lived. She loved it, even though the large rooms and high ceilings made it difficult to maintain.

A little while later, Mrs Prescott arrived in the entrance hall where some guests were preparing to depart. She looked much brighter; and with an air of controlled excitement, Lexie thought and wondered what had brought it about. Perhaps the letter was welcome good news.

'I'll pop down to the bank as soon as they're open,' she said, returning to the reception desk having seen the guests off the premises, eagerly showing her mother the cheque she'd accepted.

'All right, dear. But I have something — '

A guest approached, causing another interruption, and then the telephone rang, so Mrs Prescott never did get round to finishing what she was going to say. It would have to wait until morning coffee break; that was the time they usually managed to have ten minutes to discuss anything of importance. Lexie headed for the bank thinking about their present dilemma, and wondered when she ought to inform her mother how precarious their position was. Now she had the bank manager's ultimatum, perhaps she had better broach the subject while her mother was in a good mood.

After presenting the cheque at the bank, she hurried to the indoor market to buy fresh vegetables for lunch. Food was cheaper as well as fresher at the market, she thought, and she did like to give the guests the best they could afford. She greeted the stall holders, who recognised her as a regular, and enjoyed a few minutes' chat about the weather.

Walking down the steps into the street, she bumped into an old school friend who detained her with news about her forthcoming wedding. She was excited, wanting Lexie to hear every minute detail from the number of bridesmaids she was having to what they were going to eat at the wedding breakfast. She gave Lexie no opportunity to escape, much as she wanted to, and the carrier bags full of shopping grew heavier and heavier. Lexie finally managed to wish her well and escape. Glancing at her watch, she sighed. She would have to hurry if she was to be in time to prepare the morning coffee.

She scurried in the back door and deposited the shopping on the kitchen table. Cook came from the store cupboard, winked and said conspiratorially, 'Your mother's got a visitor — a man.'

'So?' said Lexie. 'Have you taken him some coffee?'

'Nope,' came the reply. 'Your mother said he would wait until you arrived.' With a martyred expression, she exclaimed magnanimously, 'I've taken the residents theirs, though.'

'Thanks,' Lexie said, shedding her coat and quickly combing her hair into some semblance of order with her fingers. Picking up the tray already prepared with cups and saucers instead of the usual beakers, she headed for their sitting room. 'Know what they call this mystery guest by any chance?' she called out.

Cook shook her head and went back to her baking. 'Nobody tells me anything around here, you know that,' she mumbled.

Lexie sighed, wondering if the pastry was going to be edible, and then began to think about the mysterious visitor. For one dreadful moment, she wondered if it was the bank manager.

'Ah, there you are, Lexie dear.' Her mother, looking flushed, moved some papers so Lexie could place the tray on the coffee table. A middle-aged gentleman had risen to his feet immediately she entered, and as their eyes met Lexie sensed a vague feeling of familiarity. She couldn't pinpoint what it was, but she had a strange sense of déjà vu.

'Jessica has just been telling me all about you,' he said, removing his spectacles and polishing them with visibly shaking hands.

Lexie lowered her gaze. Having noted his sun-tanned appearance, she immediately recalled the letter with the South African postmark. Was he the writer? Surely not. The letter had only arrived that morning. He seemed pleasant enough; although his face was gaunt and lined, his smile was genuine. His quality suit fitted loosely about his spare frame, and he had a most intriguing foreign accent that was quite distinctive.

'Lexie darling, we have so much to tell you. I don't know where to begin,' her mother said excitedly. 'Everything's happening so quickly. I wanted to tell you earlier, before Alex arrived, but . . . Lexie, love, I want you to meet Alex — Alex Thornton. This is going to be a shock, I know, and there's no easy way of telling you, so I'll come straight out with it. I think you'd better sit down first, though. The thing is, Alex is your father.'

Lexie's eyes widened in surprise and consternation. She stared at her mother's companion, suddenly recognising the face from an old faded photograph in her mother's bedroom. How could he be here? He was dead.

'I hope you'll not be cross with me,' her mother was saying. 'I tried to tell you the minute I got Alex's letter, but . . . well . . . '

'What . . . How . . . Why now?' Lexie stammered. She couldn't remember why she thought he was dead. She'd grown used to it over the years, so something must have been said to lead her to that assumption.

'Please, darling — I should have explained all this a long time ago, but somehow the right occasion never arose and you never asked,' her mother continued. 'Time just slipped by. Your grandma always intimated your father was dead, and I didn't correct her. She felt it made the situation more bearable — more acceptable somehow, and I didn't think there was any harm in it, since I never expected to see Alex again.' She paused and smiled at him. 'We met by chance at a party. It was love at first sight for both of us — wasn't it, Alex? But unfortunately Alex was married at the time — to Lynette.'

'Somewhat unhappily I'm afraid, but still married,' added the man, resuming his place on the settee. 'Lynette and I were living separate lives to all intents and purposes, but when I told her I wanted a divorce she hit the roof, screaming she would rather kill herself than go through all that again.'

'It was terrible.' Lexie's mother turned to look at him as if remembering the event all over again. 'She stormed out of the house and drove away in a terrible temper, not in any fit state to drive, but we couldn't stop her. We did try, but she was completely out of control. A few hours later, we heard

11

there had been an accident and she was in hospital. The car had inexplicably left the road on a bend — probably because she was going too fast, the police thought. The injuries and disablement she sustained she of course blamed us for.'

'It wasn't your fault in any way, Jessica,' Alex said, patting her hand consolingly. 'Maybe I didn't handle it very well — she was always highly strung. Anyway, Lexie, the upshot was I couldn't leave her. She already had a child by a previous marriage, so she relied on me for support. And your mother, bless her . . . Jessica said she understood. I was trapped.'

'It wouldn't have been right, Alex. She needed you, and you also had your career to think about. You know it was the only thing you could do.'

'If I had known about . . . I would never have gone — never have left you, and with our child to bring up alone. You should have told me!'

Lexie's mother's voice rose to meet

his. 'How could I? It was only after Lynette's accident I realised I was . . . and you'd already left!'

'Do you mean all these years you knew nothing about me?' Lexie said, snatching her parents' attention. The room fell silent.

'That's right,' said Alex, shaking his head sadly. 'The first I knew I had a daughter was an hour ago. I'm still trying to take it in.'

'Alex's letter was delayed in the post. I should have received it over a week ago,' her mother said whilst dealing with the cafétiere and pouring the coffee.

'After the accident we both felt terribly guilty,' Alex added, 'and since I was due to fly out almost immediately, we agreed to make a clean break.' He stopped, staring alternately at Lexie and the wall behind her, but not quite seeming to find what he sought.

'We made a pact never to contact each other,' her mother continued. 'It seemed the only way to absolve ourselves, although none of it was, I believe, our fault. Anyway, there it is; now you know the whole story, love. Alex trapped in a marriage he couldn't get out of — he worked for Lynette's father — and I never met anyone who could take his place.' Her mother smiled smugly. 'She's turned out all right, don't you think — our daughter?'

'She's beautiful,' was all Alex could say, his voice turning husky with emotion.

'So why have you come here now?' asked Lexie, speaking more sharply than she intended.

Alex appeared not to notice the censure in her voice. 'Lynette died a little over six months ago. I became a free man, but I wasn't sure if I should come back and rake up the past. I didn't know whether I would be welcome should I feel able to look up old friends; whether Jess would . . . but now I'm very glad I did. So very glad.'

'You two obviously have a lot to say to each other, so I'd better leave you to it.' Lexie quickly got to her feet. 'I must go and help with the lunches, as Cook has an appointment this afternoon and needs to be away early. See you both later.'

She fled to her bedroom, needing five minutes on her own to come to terms with things before returning to the more immediate matter of feeding the guests. Freshening up her make-up and brushing her hair, she gazed at her image in the small dressing table mirror and superimposed that of Alex Thornton — her father, with his thin face and grey-green eyes. Her father — she couldn't take it in. With a final tug with the brush flicking the ends of her hair under, she took a deep breath and left the room. Duty called, but today it was the last thing she felt like doing.

All the time she spent preparing the vegetables for lunch, she thought about Alex Thornton — her father. Now she knew where she got her green eyes from. She had often wondered, because they were so unusual with her ash-blond hair. Her father's were more grey than green, but still . . .

Somehow she managed to get on with the necessary work and helped Cook prepare a special meal for her mother and Alex to have on their own. She wondered what was going to happen now. Would they be getting married? If they did, would they go and live in South Africa? She wheeled the trolley into the sitting room, but said she still had things to do and would join them later. Somehow she was still having difficulty in accepting the fact she now had a father, and also her mother was so obviously overjoyed to see him. Would she have felt the same if it had been her in similar circumstances? she wondered. Would she have remained faithful to one man all those years? Would she ever find such a man?

By the time lunches were over, it was past two o'clock. Rejoining her parents, she waved a bottle of champagne a grateful guest had given them as a present the previous Christmas. She thought she should in some way make reparation for her less than welcoming greeting of the earth-shaking news that morning — for her mother's sake if nothing else.

'I thought perhaps we ought to be celebrating, don't you think?'

'I'll drink to that,' said Alex, springing up to help her with the glasses.

'You'll need it to fortify yourselves for when you have to run the gauntlet out there,' she added dryly. 'They're all agog about Mum's mysterious visitor. You've certainly set their tongues wagging. Miss Newsome's had a field day.'

'I can well imagine!' laughed Jessica girlishly. 'Miss Newsome is the ringleader of the residents — the real know-it-all,' she explained to Alex. 'We've certainly given them something to think about and no mistake. She claims to be able to see the future.'

'Shall we let them wait a while?' said

Alex with a lazy smile. 'At least until Jake arrives?'

'Who's Jake?' asked Lexie, looking puzzled.

'Sorry, I should have told you. Jake is my stepson. He's in hotel management, so you two should have a lot in common. He said he would come over as soon as he could make it, but it may take a day or two.'

'Where is he at the moment, in South Africa?'

'No. He owns a hotel over in the Lake District. At present he's pretty busy with a conference being held there.'

'It must be quite a large place then.'

'Fairly big. It was a bit run down, so he bought it cheaply a few years ago and he's been modernising it ever since.'

'How wonderful,' Lexie said, cringing with jealousy.

'Do you think we could all escape this evening somewhere, have a meal and get to know one another?' suggested Alex tentatively.

# 2

Lexie showered and dried her hair, leaving it to curl gently about her shoulders. It was too strong and bouncy to hold a sophisticated style, and she preferred it casual, which saved on hairdressing bills. Her dress was if anything a little on the loose side, she noticed as she pulled up the zip; she must have lost weight recently, which wasn't surprising. Still, the dress suited her, she thought, twirling round excitedly. Pale tangerine, slim-fitting, it had an attractively scalloped neckline edged with fancy motifs and a hip-hugging skirt flaring out at the hemline. Along with her high-heeled sandals and evening bag, she felt she was as ready as she was ever going to be. It made a pleasant change getting dressed up for an evening out, and she smiled at her reflection in the mirror thinking she didn't look too bad, considering.

Approaching their sitting room, she heard voices, one a stranger's, and she wondered who else her mother could possibly be entertaining, hoping and praying it wasn't one of her charlatan friends. She felt certain it wasn't Alex. It didn't sound like his voice. It was deeper and more confident. She was in two minds about entering, but decided time was marching on and they should be on their way.

'Ah, there you are, dear,' her mother said. 'I was about to call you. Come and meet Jake. He's just arrived. Jake is Alex's stepson, you remember. We didn't expect him quite so soon, did we?'

The formidable figure who levered himself from the armchair made Lexie gape in consternation. He moved with the grace and athleticism of a marauding cat, and his perceptive gaze swept over her in an almost insolent manner. She knew immediately what he thought of her appearance — her unfashionable dress and her casual hairstyle. How quaint, how dull. The dismissive, supercilious look summed it up perfectly.

'How do you do,' she stammered, blushing like a teenager. 'This seems to be the day for surprises and no mistake.'

'Sorry to come unannounced, but I gather you do have a vacancy.' The voice was rich and warm and he smiled with his eyes; dark, honey-brown eyes that bored into her with a swift measured glance. She had always thought she was tall for a woman, but he made her feel petite as his hand swallowed hers in an enthusiastic grip. He had a presence — an aura about him that left her feeling like an immature schoolgirl. She could feel the powerful strength of an athlete in his firm handshake as she floundered for words. On the other hand, her mother was looking unbelievably calm and serene.

'Will you bring Jake along to the

Royal when he's ready?' her mother asked. 'Alex booked the table for seven-thirty, so we ought to be going. We've put Jake in number seventeen.'

'Yes, of course. I'll show you to your room,' Lexie said, almost falling over herself as she turned abruptly, trying to avoid Jake's proximity.

'We'll see you both shortly then.'

Jake picked up his holdall and followed Lexie from the room. Going up in the lift, Lexie felt gauche and diffident and wished she had used the stairs. He was obviously more than capable of managing the two flights. She couldn't help noticing his expensive tweed jacket and slacks, his Rolex watch and Italian hand-made shoes. It made her all the more critical of her own off-the-peg dress, which only moments earlier had pleased her so. In the confined space he seemed more impressive than ever and she edged away from him nervously.

'I'll meet you downstairs when you're ready shall I?' she muttered quickly, showing him his allotted room.

'I won't keep you long,' he retorted with a fleeting smile.

Lexie scuttled up to her room and looked again at her appearance. She wished now she'd had the presence of mind to put her hair up — it would have made her look more mature — but it was too late for that. It always took her ages to pin it up, and she never felt comfortable with it. She grimaced at her reflection and decided to take a large mohair cape instead of her coat; that at least would look more elegant even if she perished with cold on the way.

She spent a few minutes at the reception desk unnecessarily rearranging some brochures, trying to control her nervous apprehension. The thought of dining out with her new-found father and now his stepson had made her uptight, and Jake's reappearance did nothing to bolster her self-confidence. He'd changed into a superbly tailored charcoal grey suit and white silk shirt which had all the hallmarks of having cost more than her whole wardrobe put together. His dark brown hair curling over his collar gave him a boyish look, but was belied by the firm decisive jawline. Lexie summed up Jake Thornton as probably being a pretty tough customer when roused.

'I'm sorry to keep you,' he said, opening the front door for her.

Soon they were entering the imposing foyer of the Royal Hotel the first time Lexie had set foot in Ravenstone's most prestigious hotel — and joined Alex and her mother already comfortably ensconced in the lounge bar. They were straightaway led into the dining room to a pleasant table in the window. Lexie felt tense sitting next to her newfound step-brother, so she glanced outside. It was growing dark, but she could see the bay curving round to the lighthouse and the fairy-lights along the promenade swaying in the light breeze. She could almost see Bay View except for some tall trees that got in the way.

The appearance of their waiter with the menus gave Lexie time to calm the butterflies in her stomach. Casually looking across the table at her parents, she thought how right they looked together: her father in a stylish navy-blue suit, and her mother for once conservatively dressed in a simple beige two-piece enlivened by a patterned multi-coloured blouse. By the time they had ordered and drinks procured, she felt calmer.

'I'm glad you two have met,' Alex said. 'Both being in the same line of business, you should get on well together.'

Lexie very much doubted it, judging by the expensive clothes Jake was wearing and the easy manner in which he wore them; he was in a different class altogether, but at least it gave her something to talk about. She felt very conscious of her cheap dress and surreptitiously tugged at the hemline under the table. 'Alex said you had a conference in,' she said. 'How come you've managed to leave now?'

'My staff can handle it,' he answered impassively. 'No sense in keeping a dog and barking yourself, is there?' To which there were broad smiles all round. 'I also have a capable under-manager to cope in my absence, although not for much longer I'm afraid. He's off to London at the end of the month.'

'How long have you been in this country?' Lexie asked, feeling distinctly peeved by his flippant reply.

'I came over here five years ago after my grandfather died. I was training to be an engineer so I could follow in Alex's footsteps, but when grandfather left me some money I decided to travel and see something of the world. Since I was an Englishman by birth, I began my travels here and got no further. I was brought up not far from here, I understand. Where did you say we lived, Alex?'

'At the other side of town. Out on the York road.'

'It was a lovely old house,' added Jessica. 'It's now a nursing home, I believe.'

'You were born about twenty miles away, though — on a farm, and lived there until you were two. Your mother brought you to Ravenstone when she got divorced.'

'Anyway,' continued Jake, 'I arrived in this country, and after a stint in London seeing the sights, I met this guy who told me the Lake District was the most beautiful place on earth. I didn't believe him of course, but decided to take a look-see out of curiosity. But he was right. I fell in love with the area. Have you ever been there?'

Lexie shook her head.

'There was this old family-run hotel on the market,' Jake continued. 'Just ripe for modernisation. So I took a chance and snapped it up. I've been upgrading it ever since, installing all the usual refinements — swimming pool, multi-gym, etcetera, as well as comfortable bedrooms of course. We've about finished now, so you know where to come if you fancy a holiday any time.'

'I can certainly recommend Thornton Grange,' said Alex. 'Jake's done a splendid job.'

'You do have a much longer season over there, don't you?' Lexie said rather pointedly, feeling distinctly uncomfortable at the disparity in their respective hotels.

'For sure we do. The Lake District is a great place to explore, whatever the weather or time of year, so indeed we're very fortunate. Now we never close. Christmas is one of our busiest times. How about Bay View? Are you managing to keep the wolf from the door?' he said with a wry smile.

'More or less,' she murmured.

'You two aren't talking shop, are you?' Her mother, being unusually perceptive, came to the rescue. 'This is supposed to be a celebration. It's a pity you weren't here a month earlier and we could have celebrated Lexie's birthday too.'

'Belated birthday greetings, Lexie,' Jake said, raising his glass. 'How many does that make it?'

'I'm twenty,' she muttered. 'Another year before I officially get the key of the door.'

'Well, at least we'll have time to arrange something really special for your next birthday.' Turning again to Alex, Jake said, 'Do I take it congratulations are in order, or am I being a little premature? From where I'm sitting, I can hear wedding bells already.'

Jessica blushed and Alex squeezed her hand.

'How did you two meet?' Jake asked.

'We met at a party,' said Jessica, looking delightfully coy. 'I hadn't really wanted to go, but my current boyfriend persuaded me against my better judgement. I wanted to end our relationship but found it difficult telling him. During the evening, he began drinking and became abusive; and Alex, my knight in shining armour, came to my rescue. He was there with Lynette.'

'Not that you would have noticed,' added Alex. 'Lynette was doing her usual trick of completely ignoring me, and spent the whole time with any eligible male who would entertain her. I spotted Jess looking uncomfortable and suggested a spot of fresh air might be beneficial. One thing led to another. I saw her home, and we spent as much time together as we could over the next six weeks.'

'That was the best Christmas I ever knew,' Jessica said softly. 'The only thing that spoilt it was the knowledge you were leaving in January.'

'Mother had her accident on New Year's Day, didn't she?' Jake said thoughtfully.

'That's right. And I flew out to South Africa three weeks later. You and your mother followed on a month after that.'

Lexie felt pleasantly relaxed as they walked back to Bay View, splitting into pairs quite naturally. Jake adapted his stride to suit hers.

'I could tell you felt uncomfortable back there at one stage. I guessed you were thinking about my mother, right?' Jake raised an eyebrow questioningly.

'Yes, I was,' she said, pulling her wrap tightly around her as a cool breeze blew in off the sea. She wanted to know more about her father's side of the family but didn't want to appear nosy.

'I ought to put you in the picture as to how it was between mother and Alex,' Jake said. 'You have no need be upset on my mother's behalf. For a long time I wondered why we left England so suddenly. I was only ten years old at the time, but I remember some of the trauma of her accident and the subsequent upheaval. Leaving friends and changing schools was unsettling to say the least, but when she was well enough to travel we went to South Africa to stay with my grandparents.

'Mother spent a few weeks recuperating, but then insisted we should be with Alex. I had no objections. I admired him tremendously and I was delighted to travel the country with him — until I was parcelled off to boarding school. There was never any love shown between Alex and my mother. They didn't even share a bedroom.

'Then one day I overheard my mother shrieking at him about someone called Jessica, and speaking in a most derogatory tone. She ranted on and on about how she'd ruined her life. I had never heard of anyone by that name, so when we were next alone I asked Alex who Jessica was. He was openly honest, and told me she was the love of his life whom he'd given up to take care of my mother and me.

'I couldn't believe anyone could deliberately spoil other people's lives like my mother obviously enjoyed doing. She was plain vindictive. She didn't want Alex — she didn't love him, she admitted that quite candidly. She used him — punished him.'

A car passed by, and in the flash of headlights Lexie saw his eyes narrow, his face taking on a bleak uncompromising look. Icily he murmured, 'Like she used everybody, me included. I know it's not the done thing to say anything bad about the dead, but even though she was my mother, I can't with any honesty say she was ever a warm, loving individual. Not like I imagine Jessica is. Alex didn't deserve to be so badly treated; he hadn't done anything so terrible.'

'How badly was she disabled?' asked Lexie cautiously. He obviously felt considerable contempt for his mother and she shivered at such an unhappy situation.

'She couldn't walk much — or so she made out, and of course was never able to drive again. I know she wasn't able to do a whole lot for herself, but she made out it was a lot worse than it really was — she never even tried. After all she had brought it upon herself. She acted the invalid and had everyone running around after her like a queen bee. She played on it until I suspect everyone despised her.'

Jake stopped for a moment and leaned on the railing which guarded a steep drop down to the lower promenade. He stared out to sea as if scanning the horizon. He appeared to have forgotten Lexie was there, so she remained silent, not sure what to say. She stood by his side trying not to shiver, glad that it was a fine, clear night and Ravenstone was looking at its best.

'I have a great deal to thank Alex for, especially as he's no blood relation,' Jake said finally, turning towards her with a sigh. 'He's been more like a father to me than I could have expected. He's had a desperately hard time and I'll do anything I can to make life easier for him now.'

'What about your own father?' she asked. 'What happened to him?'

'He died when I was about seven. I don't remember much about him. After the divorce, which I gather was extremely acrimonious, he emigrated to Australia. Alex has been my father to all intents and purposes. I took his surname when my mother married him, which is perhaps the only thing she did that I'm grateful to her for.'

'You've had quite a traumatic life from all accounts,' she said lightly.

'It's not been all bad, but Mother got even more demanding after Grandfather died. I thought Alex a brick to put up with it. I got out and came to England, but he stayed with her right to the end. He told me he'd grown immune to her callous attitude, but it left its mark. It took its toll on his health, and he's only now starting to recover. He's quite a guy, your father, believe you me.' Then he noticed Lexie's pale face reflected in the moonlight. 'Hey, you'll catch your death of cold. Come along; it's time I saw you home.' Tucking her arm in his, they walked briskly back to Bay View.

In bed that night, despite the lateness of the hour, Lexie couldn't sleep. Jake had upset her equilibrium by his sheer masculinity and maturity. Ten years made a lot of difference by all accounts. He had an air of quiet confidence which she seemed to be sadly lacking at the moment. If only she had been able to convince the bank manager he could trust her — that Bay View would soon be a viable concern again — but she hadn't. He obviously saw her as too young and incompetent, which on the face of it she was. This was all her fault. She pounded the pillow. There must be a way out of their predicament, there had to be. Now it was more urgent than ever to find it.

# 3

'Just what do you think you're doing?'
Lexie's eyes blazed with fury on
discovering Jake seated at the open
writing desk.

'What does it look like I'm doing?'

'How dare you go through my private
papers? The running of this hotel has
nothing to do with you.'

Jake leaned nonchalantly back in the
chair, precariously balancing it on two
legs, waving the letter from the bank
manager and totally ignoring her tirade.
'I was looking for some writing paper
and found this. How are you going to
deal with it?'

'That has nothing to do with you. You
had no right to poke your nose into our
affairs.' Lexie snatched the offending
letter from his outstretched hand.
'There's writing paper in your room.'

'I happened to be down here when I

37

required some. I didn't break any locks or anything. I wasn't snooping.' Tipping his head to one side, he peered at her through half-closed eyes. 'Does your mother know how serious things are?'

'No, no she doesn't, so don't you go upsetting her. I'll find a way of getting the money,' she snapped.

Was that the truth? he wondered. He was half inclined to believe her. 'I had no intention of doing so. But what are you going to do about it? Christmas isn't far away; it doesn't give you long.'

'Just stay out of it.' Lexie was shaking with rage and close to panic. She knew only too well how precarious their position was and she didn't need Jake's ruthless assessment rubbing it in. She was getting to the end of her tether.

'Lexie.' He rose to his feet and stood intimidatingly close, resting his hands on her shoulders. 'Please don't get me wrong. I merely want to help. I told you, I don't want Alex upset, and besides he hasn't got the resources to help you out of this predicament.'

'I never thought of asking him,' Lexie cried, her eyes brimming with tears. After all that had happened recently, she was beginning to feel like driftwood being swept along by the tide soon to be washed up on the shore alone and penniless. Now her mother had Alex, maybe it was time she found a place of her own. She was almost at her wits' end, and she didn't need this pompous opinionated individual gloating over her troubles. 'I am quite capable of dealing with it,' she muttered. 'Being my father's stepson doesn't give you the right to delve into our affairs.'

'Look, I really do want to help,' he said in a sympathetic tone. 'Can't we discuss this calmly without involving either of your parents? I'm sorry if you think I was being unduly inquisitive, but one can tell things aren't too rosy here.'

He glanced round the small sitting room and Lexie knew exactly what he was thinking — seeing the frayed carpet, the shabby furnishings and the wallpaper that should have been replaced years ago. It was plain for all to see and obviously hadn't missed his keen-eyed observation.

'Yes, well . . . Now you've seen for yourself the state we're in . . . ' Lexie clenched her hands and desperately tried to hold back the tears that pricked her eyelids. 'Why don't you go back to your magnificent showplace and leave us alone. It's my problem, not yours, and I'll solve it in my own good time.'

'Why you and not your mother?' he asked. 'It's quite a responsibility for someone of your age. Finance is a complicated business.'

She shook her head wearily. 'I would have thought it was obvious. Finance is hardly my mother's forte. Gran used to do the book-work and she instructed me, so when she died I automatically carried on. I am twenty, you know, not a teenager, and have grown up in the hotel trade.'

'You look as if you've had a tough time recently,' he remarked. 'What really caused the problem? Feel like unburdening yourself?' Tipping her chin up with his index finger, he gazed into her eyes.

She saw tactful compassion, and crumpled under his troubled face. It was the final straw — in her tightly bottled-up emotional state, she collapsed. He knew anyway, so what difference would it make? It was a relief to tell someone. She slumped down on the settee, wiping away tears with the back of her hand.

'We've had a few poor years recently in quick succession and last winter we were badly hit by the storms battering our coastline. I don't know about you, but here we get a stiff north-easterly wind which causes havoc every once in a while. It was our bad luck it happened last year. Our insurance cover was less than adequate to pay for the repair work and, of course, like most resorts along this coast, visitors aren't coming as they used to. They're all going on package tours abroad or to health farms and hotels with sports facilities,' she gibed. 'Many former hotels in Raven-stone are now flats, nursing homes or residential homes for the elderly, that sort of thing, as a means of making them pay. The trend for the traditional family holiday by the sea has changed, as you're probably well aware.'

He nodded and shrugged his shoulders. 'How come the insurance company wouldn't pay in full?'

Lexie went red. 'I . . . I . . . The premiums were so high.' Dry-mouthed, she whispered, 'I'd let the cover lapse while I sought out a new arrangement.'

'Hmm,' was all he said, but it was enough.

'All right, I know, it was a mistake. You don't need to rub it in. It was a stupid thing to do.'

Jake didn't say anything, but prowled round the room with hands in pockets, ending up by the window. 'What's your opinion of the market?' he asked abruptly. 'Do you see Bay View making its way as a hotel, or would it be better to turn it into flats?'

'If money was no object,' she replied, thankful he'd not taunted her incompetence, 'it would obviously be preferable to turn it into flats. We have the advantage of splendid sea views, and it would easily convert I think, although I'm not an architect. We applied for planning permission a couple of years ago, but the cost was prohibitive. We couldn't afford it then and we can't now. The bank manager isn't being very co-operative. I'll have to see if I can extend the mortgage again somehow,' she went on miserably. 'Or maybe I can convince Mum it's time to put it up for sale. I need time to think. I only got that letter the other day, and since then things have been a little traumatic to say the least.'

She sat with a bowed head, hugging herself in an effort not to cry. She wouldn't allow him to see the depths to which she had plummeted. In some way, talking it over with him had helped clarify in her own mind what had to be done — what she had known all along she had to do. She would need to discuss it with her mother soon, but she knew it was going to be an unhappy decision. Bay View was the only home either of them had ever known.

Jake turned his back on the view, propped himself up against the sideboard, and folded his arms. 'From what I've seen, I think you're quite correct in your assessment.' He studied her for a moment, well aware of the tension in her. 'What would you say to me putting up the finance to do the necessary alterations to turn it into flats?'

Her head jolted up. 'How could . . . ? Why should you?' she asked, staring at him in disbelief. 'It has nothing to do with you.'

'I told you I want what's best for Alex. He should have inherited under my mother's will, but she only bequeathed him a miserly sum. After all he had put up with and all he had done for her over the years, Mother left the bulk of the estate to a female cousin who had

44

latched on to her latterly,' Jake said sourly, his mouth curled in disgust. 'Mother left me the house in South Africa because she knew I didn't want it and had no wish to return there. I told you she was vindictive,' he went on grimly.

'Since I was preoccupied with my own business at the time, Alex took care of things out there for me. He stayed on after the funeral, put the house up for sale, dealt with the solicitors and generally wound everything up, but by then he was quite ill. Reaction, I shouldn't wonder. He's been staying at Thornton Grange during this last summer, but flew back to finalise everything mainly on my behalf. Now it's resolved, the money from the sale of the house I could use here. It would be a rather gratifying way to utilise my mother's inheritance.'

'But how would you recover your money?' she asked, wondering if this was indeed a way out of her troubles. 'I couldn't possibly . . . '

'On reflection, I think it would be useful to have a flat in Ravenstone. I could take over the top floor once it's converted, and the ground floor could be made into a pleasant flat for Alex and Jessica. That would still leave at least two and possibly three flats to sell or lease to suitable occupants.'

'So as a business venture it could be sound in your view?' Lexie's mind was ticking over feverishly, thinking of problem areas. If they managed to sell the flats at a good price, it could work. It sounded plausible, but she wondered where the catch was; there usually was at least one.

'I think it would. However, there would have to be one or two conditions attached to my putting forward such a large amount of cash.'

'I wouldn't expect otherwise.' Lexie, despite her youth, realised nobody did anything for nothing these days, especially someone of Jake's calibre. At least he was giving her an alternative, which was more than the bank manager was willing to do. Now came the snag. She wasn't sure whether she could bear to hear it. Having had her spirits raised, she didn't want them dashed so soon.

'The main condition would be that it was strictly between the two of us. Agreed?'

'Oh yes, of course if possible,' she concurred. 'I don't want either of them to know how serious the financial position is if I can help it. I know I've been a complete fool, but so far I've managed to keep the seriousness of the situation from my mother. It's something I have to resolve. I got us into this mess and I have to find a solution. What other conditions would there be?'

'Just one.' He paused and looked directly at her, his eyes mesmerising in their intensity as if he was trying to hypnotise her.

Lexie found she couldn't look away. She was holding her breath waiting for the axe to fall. Waiting for the moment when the deal fell through because she couldn't accept his final proposal.

'I want you to come and work for me at Thornton Grange.'

'What! Why?' she stammered, taken completely by surprise again. He had the knack of perplexing her until she didn't know what she was doing or saying. 'I don't understand. Why would you want me at your hotel?'

'I don't suppose you will want to live here permanently once they get back from their honeymoon, will you?' he said, his eyes twinkling good humouredly.

'No . . . but . . . No, I thought about looking for another position in Ravenstone. Perhaps a live-in job as a housekeeper, or rent a flat and get a job at the sports centre.' She hadn't really given it much thought and had no idea what sort of employment she could get, but said the first thing that came into her head.

'Well, those are the conditions, take or leave it,' he said, obviously expecting an answer immediately.

'What sort of job?' she asked, playing for time, desperately trying to think. She was confused and excited; it sounded too good to be true. It was such a truly magnificent offer, and the more she thought about it the more relieved she felt.

'Anything I decide will be suitable. All my staff can cope with any job allocated,' he declared airily. 'How about it? I'll have to be getting back. I've been away longer than I anticipated, and my under-manager is leaving soon, but I'd like to set things in motion here as soon as possible if you're agreeable. Time is of the essence.'

'You're rushing me. I don't know what to say.' Stunned by the suddenness with which all her worries would be resolved, she was also apprehensive at the thought of working for Jake. Never having worked for anybody else before, she wondered how she would cope.

'In business you often have to make

quick decisions to benefit from opportunities which arise. I presume you accept that, don't you?' He paused. 'So think about it rationally. You can't keep going like you have for much longer before they put you out on the streets, and I guess so far you haven't had much luck raising capital in the present climate. You might not like what the bank manager says, but he's correct in one thing — now is not a good time in the property market. So why not agree to my terms, and I'll make all the necessary arrangements with the bank today. You haven't got that many options open to you in reality.'

'I really don't know what to say,' Lexie repeated herself. Something was struggling at the back of her mind that Jake Thornton wasn't a man to do anything for charity, so what was in it for him? Could it be a worthwhile proposition? Did he know something she didn't? Was it revenge for his mother's behaviour, or was it something else?'

'You need a job and I'm offering you one. I don't see your problem.'

'Oh, all right,' she said rather ungraciously. 'I accept so long as you promise never to reveal to my mother how precarious things are and why.' She was relieved to have the decision more or less taken out of her hands. It would be smugly pleasing to be able to go and see the bank manager and tell him she no longer required his overdraft facility, and get him to return the deeds of the hotel which he was holding as collateral. That in itself would be well worth it.

'Good,' Jake replied calmly and matter-of-factly. He had known all along she would agree to his terms. 'Now let's get down to business. As I said, I'll have to leave in a day or two, and there's much to be done. We'll talk to Alex and Jessica tonight together. OK?'

Lexie chewed her lip and nodded weakly. She felt she was being steam-rollered into something she knew she was probably going to regret, but for the moment she couldn't see any other alternative. In any event, there was going to be a delay while the usual procedures were implemented. Time in which she could get used to the idea of no longer being her own boss.

'Don't look so apprehensive, Lexie. It'll be all right, you'll see. Today we'll go and find out if the planning permission is still valid and line up an architect and builder. I trust you to help me with local knowledge on both counts.'

★ ★ ★

The rest of the day went in a whirlwind of meetings and discussions, so by the time they were sitting down that night to talk to her parents, Lexie felt exhausted.

'Now what's all this about?' asked Alex when they were all together in the small sitting room. Alex and Jessica sat on the settee while Lexie toyed nervously with her handkerchief in one of the armchairs. Jake, who had been staring moodily out of the window, leisurely walked over and sat down in the other armchair.

'What have you two been up to? I know that look. Come on, spill the beans. You've got something up your sleeve, haven't you, son?'

Jake flashed Alex a quick smile of sympathetic understanding. 'You might say that. Lexie and I have been busy today fixing everything up, so I hope you'll go along with what we propose.'

Jessica Prescott tried unsuccessfully to catch her daughter's eye, but Lexie, feeling distinctly uncomfortable, couldn't bring herself to face anyone. Jake had more or less taken everything out of her hands with such efficiency she felt like a limp rag. Ever since she found him reading that letter, she had been in a state of constant bemusement. She hadn't given him carte blanche over her, had she, but that was how it appeared. Okay, so now he held the purse strings; but it didn't mean she was a puppet having to do everything he desired.

# 4

Jake drove along the coast road, his thoughts a mixture of surprise, suspicion and scepticism. It was good to see Alex looking so happy. He was glad in a way he had urged him to return to Ravenstone and look up old acquaintances, but also it posed a problem. He wasn't going to be taken in as readily as Alex. Granted, Jessica was perfectly charming, just as Alex remembered. But was it genuine? Was she another fortune hunter in disguise? Alex was his main concern — his only concern — and he would do whatever he felt needed doing to protect his step-father's well-being. Thankfully money wasn't a problem as such, but he was not going to be so philanthropic as to throw it away on any gold-digger no matter how charming. He'd seen what happened all too often, once coerced into taking the trip down the aisle. The speed with which they intended marrying was worrying, but Alex said it was at his insistence now he had a daughter to look out for. He idolised Lexie.

Turning off the main road, he meandered down a country lane and drew up on the grass verge. Normally his mind would be fully focused on the proposed new project. In business one had to give one hundred per cent attention to such schemes, so why now did a certain pair of green eyes keep distracting him? Hadn't he vowed never to be diverted by the female of the species after his latest embarrassing interlude? Lexie — was she the ingenuous innocent she portrayed? Surely she would have asked about her father long ago. Was it credible she believed the story that he had died? She was a capable young woman, if somewhat naive, and he wondered how she would fit in at Thornton Grange. What had possessed him to take her under his wing like that? To please

Alex, of course!

'Good grief I must need my head examined,' he muttered. Alex was so thrilled to find he had a daughter that he couldn't see beyond the end of his nose.

Jake tried to regain his application to the business in hand. Frowning, he scanned the bare fields and oriented the site plan. Maybe he should have brought Alex along; perhaps he could have made constructive suggestions. Had they got the best out of the plot? What possible snags could crop up now even at this late stage? He was having difficulty concentrating, and yet he couldn't afford to slip up. Too much was riding on this deal.

He got out of the car to stretch his legs and clear his brain, but he was soon back. He had forgotten to collect his jacket and the wind was bitingly cold. Cursing under his breath, he turned the heater on full and recalled the warmth of his childhood in sunny South Africa. Funny how little things stirred recollections. He hadn't given his childhood much thought for long enough. He had no wish to return there. He felt at home in his native country even if at times the weather could be atrocious.

With a sigh, he turned the car around and headed back to Bay View wondering what the future held for them all. He smiled when he thought about Lexie's relief and pleasure when he offered to help. He was glad to help if only because he didn't want Alex bothered about anything for the moment. He wanted him to build up his strength because he was going to need it in the New Year if all went well.

★   ★   ★

'Find alternative accommodation for your residents as quickly as possible, Lexie,' Jake commanded in his usual no-nonsense manner the next day. 'I want a start made on the ground floor flat immediately.'

'But what about the planning permission and so on?' she replied. 'We can't . . . '

'Don't wait for that,' Jake said, turning away from his observation of the sunlit bay. 'Make a start on emptying the place so the builders can move in. There's a lot they can do before the architect comes up with the final drawings. Since Jessica and Alex are coming to stay at Thornton Grange for a while, do you think you can manage on your own? It's only a matter of seeing all your residents fixed up with new accommodation and then keeping an eye on the workmen when they arrive.'

'Yes, but . . . How . . . ' she stuttered. He was like a human dynamo issuing instructions and expecting immediate response, not giving her time to marshal her thoughts or arguments.

'I've made a list of the priorities,' he said, waving to some papers on the sideboard. 'The builders can get cracking straightaway, and when the architect comes up with the initial layouts, let's have a quick response. There'll be no trouble at the town hall, they assure me. They went out of their way to be helpful, and said the application would pass with no objections.'

Lexie nodded resignedly. She couldn't wait for him to leave. He had just about taken over the running of Bay View since his arrival, and she had to go along with it to keep the peace. She wondered what the staff at Thornton Grange thought of him. If he was as bossy with them, she wondered how he managed to keep them. He spent hours on the phone each day checking up on what was happening over there, barking out instructions when necessary, but it was obvious he couldn't remain at Bay View much longer.

'Do you want me to tell the residents?' he asked. 'It shouldn't be too difficult to relocate them. I gather there are plenty of vacancies not too far from here, and it would be best to get them installed before the bad weather sets in.'

'I'll do it,' said Lexie quickly, feeling his firm bombastic attitude wouldn't go down too well. Some of them were already looking apprehensive about all the strange activity going on. She knew that rumours were rife, but so far no one had asked outright what was happening. Even the ebullient Miss Newsome had kept her counsel. She too was in awe of Jake, and Lexie had kept out of her way, not wanting to explain prematurely.

Jake left later that day and Lexie let out a long sigh of relief. She was beginning to wonder what sort of tiger she had let loose in their hotel, and her mother was too preoccupied to notice.

★   ★   ★

Two weeks later, the last of the residents left. Lexie wandered round the deserted building, going from room to room to see it for the last time in its present form before the builders started ripping it apart. It hadn't been as difficult as she had imagined re-locating everyone, but now she was alone with her thoughts — and worries. She ended up at the top of the house, in the attics where they and the staff had their rooms. This would all belong to Jake. She looked out across the windswept sands, saw the waves pounding against the breakwater, and realised how she was going to miss that oh-so-familiar view. The sun rising over the horizon tinged the clouds a delicate pink as they scurried westward. Ravenstone was beautiful — Bay View was her home — why should she have to leave? It wasn't fair.

At times like this, she wondered if she ought to have pursued other financial avenues, but she knew she hadn't any real alternative. Jake's offer was more than generous, so she had to do as he suggested, and yet . . . the thought of Jake's domineering manner made her cautious. She knew that life was never going to be the same again without a home of her own, and wondered for how long she would have to work for him before he considered the debt repaid.

The builders arrived to make a start, and later the same morning the architect found Lexie in the kitchen brewing up. 'I've brought you some plans to have a look at. See what you think. They're a bit sketchy at the moment.'

'That was quick,' she remarked, wondering why everyone jumped to do Jake's bidding. Money talking, she thought peevishly.

He accepted a cup of tea as Lexie dispensed it to the men, and then she looked at the drawings with him at the kitchen table.

'I think we should aim for three flats apart from this one and the penthouse. One large three-bedroomed on first floor and two smaller two-bedroomed ones on second floor.'

'Can we manage that and still keep them self-contained?' she queried. She couldn't see how they could achieve it without either making them far too small and poky or with no sea view, which would hardly make sense. The view was going to be their best selling point.

'Yes. I'll show you.' He unrolled the drawings and explained each floor layout. He'd obviously been very busy. Each floor had been divided up making best use of the available space. Each flat would be different, but since the lift was fairly central, they could all be self-contained.

'That looks fine,' she admitted thoughtfully. 'It should be more profit-able too, shouldn't it?' She only had a vague idea of the financial situation since Jake had taken charge of all that.

Next he showed her the plans for the penthouse which according to him was the next flat to be done, weather permitting. Obviously Jake wanted his flat useable at the earliest possible time, and after all it was his money that was footing the bill. For herself, she wanted the other flats completed speedily so they could be sold and Jake could have his money back. She only hoped they sold quickly. She hated the idea of being beholden to him for any longer than necessary.

'Gosh,' she murmured, staring at the drawings. The penthouse flat was going to be fantastic. Gone were the old-fashioned sash windows and sloping ceilings, and in their place was a mansard roof with all the front rooms having sliding windows giving access to a high-level balcony. She could well imagine sitting out there in summer having breakfast with the splendid vista of Ravenstone Bay below. What a wonderful way to start the day! Lucky old Jake. It crossed her mind to wonder how much of the time Jake would spend there when it was finished. Would it be merely a holiday flat, occupied for a few odd weeks a year? That would be a great shame. She couldn't think of a nicer place to spend one's time than Ravenstone.

* * *

They were fortunate the construction of Bay View made the alterations into self-contained flats minimal, and soon it was progressing well. Some of the larger rooms needed dividing into two, and of course a new kitchen and bathroom made in the ground floor flat. Lexie's role was to organise the decorators and then oversee the furnishing using some retained furniture her mother particularly wanted to keep for sentimental reasons. She found it quite enthralling now the work was taking shape, and pondered occasionally on who would be designing and furnishing Jake's flat on completion. She couldn't imagine him handing that over to a novice like herself. Perhaps he had a girlfriend who would be more than willing to undertake such a commission, but she didn't wish to dwell on that scenario.

She daydreamed about him often. He'd made such an impact on her, and now he wasn't there bossing her around, she could think about him more dispassionately. The meeting with her father had been memorable enough, but Jake had been something else. It wasn't just because he'd saved her from catastrophe or because he was almost a relative. Jake was such a dynamic personality, the like of which she had never encountered before.

She sighed and settled to the task of choosing wallpaper, wishing she felt more confident and attractive. Until she met Jake, she hadn't worried too much about how she looked. She hadn't spent a fortune on clothes, never having had the opportunity, but it hadn't bothered her. She usually had sufficient to make herself presentable, buying sensibly from chain stores. Now she was conscious of a lack of social grace and awareness, which made her feel uncomfortable. She began taking an interest in fashion magazines, hoping to get some tips on what the well-dressed woman was wearing, but in the end came to the conclusion everything was far too expensive. Even if she could afford it, she didn't think she could bring herself to pay such fancy prices.

The ground floor flat was going to be the largest one because of the addition of the old downstairs kitchen, which was being transformed into a bed-sitting room for Lexie. It would have its own private access to the rear garden and yet be part of Alex and Jessica's flat too. Lexie looked around her new bedroom and wondered what the future held for her. Jake had very generously arranged for her to buy whatever she deemed necessary in the way of furnishings, so she was thoroughly enjoying the experience. It had been a long time since they could afford to refurbish without making do with the cheapest possible; not that she didn't look for value for money now. She wanted to show him that she was capable of being efficient and business-like, choosing very selectively the new carpets and curtains for her parents' flat.

She decided, even though Jake was

footing the bill for the rest of the house, that when it came to her room she was going to pay for whatever it needed. She didn't want to be beholden to him for anything more than was absolutely necessary, and in the past she had always decorated her own room, so there was no reason why she shouldn't do so now. She wasn't used to being idle, and making tea for the workmen hardly constituted earning her keep.

As soon as the builders removed the kitchen equipment, transforming it into a bedroom with a large picture window and installed a glass-panelled door leading to the back garden, she made a start. Eventually there was to be a conservatory added at the back as an extra sitting-out area, but that would come later when the rest of the flats were finished. Choosing her wallpaper with care, she made a start on the painting while the plumber was busy creating a bathroom from what had been the walk-in pantry. She decided to make use of some of the newest curtains they had from the old dining room, but had turned down all the old-fashioned furniture in favour of buying something light and modern. She felt determined to show Jake she had talent. The fiasco over the insurance was an error of judgement brought about by financial constraints. She might not be as skilful as him in many ways, but she was a dab hand at interior design.

Lexie found it rather fun having so many men about the place and accepted their cheeky remarks good-naturedly. She spent a good deal of the time making tea and generally being available to lend a hand in minor ways. Jake had instructed the architect to pull out all the stops so as to have the first flat ready by Christmas, and judging by the hive of activity it looked achievable. Each morning Lexie pulled on jumper and jeans, tying her hair in a ponytail, prepared to accept whatever the day brought forth cheerfully. Now the project was underway, she was enjoying the freedom with nobody bossing her around and no one else to look after. During the day while the men were working it was a lively, noisy place, but when they left in the evening she sometimes got depressed being in the building all by herself. For the last few years, they hadn't closed during the winter, so she wasn't used to having Bay View deserted. It seemed eerie, almost ghostly. Occasionally she went along to the sports centre, but found it more nerve-wracking coming back to the empty building after dark, so she stopped going.

When one of her badminton partners rang up and asked her out for a meal, she accepted gratefully. It had been a long time since her last date, and she looked forward to it with pleasure. She sang in the shower and spent a long time choosing what to wear, feeling giddy at the prospect of an evening out, almost like a schoolgirl on her first date. When Nigel arrived she was ready, not wanting to have to invite him in with the place being such a mess.

'Punctual I see,' he remarked.

'I'm hungry,' she said, buttoning up her coat.

They walked to the restaurant along the Esplanade. She had known Nigel from her school days and enjoyed his light-hearted approach to life — he was never serious, it seemed, always ready with a witty observation or joke.

'I hear big things are afoot at Bay View. Have you come into money — won the pools or something? If you have, I don't mind helping you spend it.'

'Nothing like that,' she chuckled. 'We've decided to join the never-ending stream of hoteliers trying to make ends meet by turning the place into flats, that's all.'

'It's a sign of the times, I'm afraid. Ravenstone's changing into a geriatrics' retirement resort. People are only coming on day trips these days now that they own cars and can get here so easily, which is excellent news from my point of view. By the way, when are you going to trade in that old jalopy of yours? It must be well past its sell-by date. We've acquired an immaculate younger version with extremely low mileage. It belonged to an old biddy who only drove it a couple of miles each week to the shops. I'll let you have it at a good price. It's a snip, honestly.'

'Sorry, no can do,' she said wryly. 'The bank manager would have a fit if I even suggested it.'

'Don't mention bank managers to me!' he growled. 'They're the bane of my life. My account always seems to be in the red. I don't know where the money goes. Come on, I think you said you were starving. I'll have to work on you some other time. Let's go eat. Maybe when you're fed you'll be more co-operative.'

Lexie thoroughly enjoyed the meal. Nowadays she made do with a sandwich or something on toast most of the time, so the chicken a la crème was a positive treat. For sweet she chose the raspberry soufflé and crisp shortbread biscuits. Nigel plied her with wine until she felt her head spin, while regaling her with exaggerated stories about his work as a car salesman, embellishing his prowess to the point of absurdity. She found him an amusing companion and was definitely light-headed and giggly by the time they were ready to leave. Outside, the fresh air soon cleared her head, and they meandered back to Bay View laughing at silly recollections and exploits of their school days.

'Thank you, Nigel, for a really splendid evening,' Lexie said, inserting her key in the lock. 'I've enjoyed every minute.'

'Don't I get to come in?' he pleaded sulkily.

'Not tonight if you don't mind. I have to be up early tomorrow, and the place is in rather a mess as you can imagine. It's chaos.'

'Come on, Lexie. Now that you have the place to yourself, why not loosen up a bit. Live a little — invite me in for coffee. Go on.'

She hesitated, not wanting to appear ungrateful, and also remembering how she disliked entering the deserted building alone. He took advantage of her indecision by pushing the door open wide and urging her inside.

'Gee, it's cold outside. I could do with some coffee to warm me up. After all, I have a long walk home, you know. Couldn't bring the car — can't afford to lose my licence.'

They were in the hall before she knew it, and she was warning him to be careful where he walked as builders' equipment littered the floor. She led him into the makeshift kitchen and put the coffee on, wishing he hadn't imposed his way in like that. It had rather spoilt the evening. She felt apprehensive being alone with him in the close confines of the empty building. It made her feel vulnerable. It was the first time she had ever been alone with a man in an empty house.

Nigel had always been impetuous and brash as a schoolboy — the extrovert amongst them which she had found appealing, but now — now she wasn't too sure. Maybe it was the eeriness of Bay View which was getting to her.

'Coffee won't be long,' she said, arranging biscuits on a plate.

'How about a kiss while I'm waiting,' Nigel said, sneaking up behind her.

'Let go, Nigel,' she said, trying to sound mildly amused, although experiencing a moment of panic.

He laughed and teasingly slid his hands from her waist up over her breasts and plucked at the buttons of her blouse. This was too much. She lashed out violently with both arms and spun round to face him. 'What do you think you're doing? I said coffee — nothing else.' She broke free from his grasp only to find herself backed up against the table.

'Come now, what's a kiss between friends? You know I've always fancied you. Ever since we were at school I was attracted to you, although you never gave me a second glance. Prove you're not the ice maiden they make you out to be.'

'Who calls me an ice maiden?' she snapped, inching away sideways.

'Oh, you know, our usual crowd.'

'Simply because I don't throw myself into the arms of every guy I go out with!' she retorted, and walked away to switch off the kettle, her face red with anger.

'Well you don't exactly encourage them, do you?'

'Just because I'm choosy, that doesn't mean I'm frigid.'

'Don't you like me, Lexie?' Nigel swayed towards her and she hurriedly stepped aside to put the table between them.

'Of course I like you,' she snapped. 'I wouldn't have gone out with you otherwise.'

'Well then, what's the harm in a little cuddle and a kiss or two?'

Lexie felt her face burning. Maybe

the wine was making her dim-witted. 'I'm not in the mood, Nigel. I need an early night — I told you.'

'Is that all the thanks I get then?' he said casually, selecting a biscuit from the plate and munching it quite deliberately. 'My dates are usually more forthcoming, I must say.'

'What on earth did you expect? I said like you, Nigel, but I'm not in love with you.'

'Who said anything about being in love? Oh, forget it,' he snarled and stormed out.

She heard the front door slam so ferociously the building shook. Glumly she made herself a drink and retired to bed. It was another setback to her confidence. Was she being too choosy? Most girls of her age would be more willing, she knew, but so far she had never felt inclined to progress further than the kissing stage of a relationship. Did that mean she was frigid? she wondered.

# 5

Jake decided he ought to see how the renovations were progressing for himself. He'd had reports from Lexie and the architect, and all seemed to be going according to plan; but if he was honest, it was an excuse to see Lexie again. He didn't know why. He didn't need to visit Bay View. Lexie should be perfectly capable of dealing with the minor queries that arose. As he drove over the Pennines, he thrust to the back of his mind the fact that he felt some sort of responsibility for her. He thought of her as his step-sister, but that didn't mean he had to look out for her. No, he was going to see how his investment was taking shape, because that was what it was — an investment, pure and simple.

He really must try to locate another under-manager so he could have a holiday, but that wasn't too pressing. It would be merely a change from routine and a necessity, or so he'd been told to recharge the batteries. He gunned the car down the outside lane of the motorway, conscious his miscellaneous thoughts were leading him along paths he'd rather not take. Lexie — his step-sister. Or was she? He didn't want to think such disloyal thoughts, but they still nagged away at him occasionally.

★   ★   ★

'When you've finished your tea, do you think you could give me a hand in the shower?' Andy the plumber asked Lexie. 'My mate hasn't turned up. Another night on the tiles I wouldn't wonder,' he said, shaking his head ruefully. 'What it is to be young and fearless!'

'Sure thing — show me what you want me to do,' Lexie said blithely, ignoring the ribald remarks from the decorators. 'It will be lovely having my own shower working.'

'If you'll hold on to that for a moment, there's one more joint needs seeing to and then it should be all complete . . . There that does it,' Andy said as he nipped up the last bolt. Now, hey presto. Water I hope. Keep your fingers crossed.'

There was a sudden spurt as an air lock in the pipes cleared twisting the shower head round and water shot out, drenching them both in the process. Andy grabbed hold of Lexie as she started to slide on the slippery surface, and both were laughing gleefully. Their hilarity was ended abruptly by the sarcastic comment from the doorway.

'So this is what you get up to! I usually take my clothes off to have a shower.'

'Jake! What are you doing here? Why didn't you let us know you were coming?' Lexie spluttered. 'You weren't expected.'

'Obviously!'

His disgust at the state she was in and his acerbic comment made her flinch with embarrassment. 'Andy's mate hasn't turned up, so I was giving him a hand.' She tried unsuccessfully to subdue her mirth.

'If you can tear yourself away from such childish behaviour, I want to talk to you.' He stalked out in a huff.

'Hey, I'm sorry,' said Andy. 'I didn't mean to get you into hot water.'

'Not so hot!' Lexie giggled. 'Think nothing of it. He's an old grouch. I'm glad to see my shower is now operational. Now I can really make some headway down here. I'd better go tidy myself up, though, for the boss.'

Jake glowered when she reappeared as if he'd overheard her flippant remark. 'What on earth have you been up to in here?' he asked, waving his hand in the air. 'You've even got paint in your hair.'

Lexie pulled off the rubber band and

unthreaded her plait. 'I've been decorating my room. What do you think to it?'

'I thought the decorators were starting down here next week, or so you said.'

'Yes they are — to do the rest of the flat, but I always decorate my own room,' she said, standing with hands on hips admiring her handiwork.

'There was no need for that.'

'There was every need for that,' she retorted, wanting to state her point clearly. She didn't want him thinking she was a mercenary individual out for all she could get. 'I'm beholden to you enough already, so whatever I can do myself I will, all right?'

'That's the way you see it, is it?' he remarked, quietly kicking himself. He'd been feeling sorry for her and here she was having the time of her life. He ought to have known. She was an attractive women in a house full of randy workmen. Didn't she have any sense? Didn't she realise even dressed in workaday clothes, she was still very appealing to the opposite sex? She looked as if she'd led a sheltered life and had no idea what dangers lurked in the big wide world. She was standing there squaring her shoulders, quite openly belligerent, her hair a shaggy tangle; and yet in a way the wildness of it appealed. It gave her an air of playful youthfulness and made him feel the ten-year age gap insurmountable. He couldn't ever remember feeling young. He had grown up quickly after his mother's accident; she had seen to that. He was the man of the house, she kept saying, disregarding Alex — her husband.

'Yes, it is,' Lexie was saying. 'Now, I'll go and tidy myself if you wouldn't mind waiting. The water was rather cold.' She left without waiting for a reply and went up to the room she was using as a bedroom. Routing out a skirt and a clean jumper, she spent a few minutes searching for a pair of shoes which for some reason had escaped out of sight under the wardrobe, and then after applying a dab of lipstick hurried back down. 'Sorry to keep you.'

Jake was prowling round her parents' flat inspecting everything as if with a fine-tooth comb. The atmosphere about the place had changed perceptively. Usually the men whistled and sang as they worked — they were a happy bunch, but now they were silent except for the hammering and banging necessary to do their jobs.

'You seem to be doing OK,' Jake admitted grudgingly, which to Lexie felt like praise indeed.

'Thank you, kind sir,' she replied, cheekily dipping into a mock curtsey.

His eyebrows met in deep brooding frown. 'Grab a coat; I'll take you out to lunch. We can't talk here.'

Since she was hungry, who was she to refuse? Maybe he'd set off without breakfast and his temper would improve once he'd eaten. In a little Italian restaurant just off the High Street, as soon as they had placed their order, he fired question after question about progress on the job. Had she received the relevant paperwork from the Town Hall? Had she contacted the manufacturer about servicing the lift? Had the builder delivered the updated drawings showing the revised layout of the top flat? Once he seemed satisfied with her answers, she relaxed a little. His unfriendly manner was most unsettling, and his ability always to look immaculately turned out rather annoying. She knew her hair was probably a mess after its soaking; she hadn't had time to do more than clip it into a ponytail when she returned to her room. She had got out of the way of dressing up recently and suddenly realised how scruffy she must have appeared.

'I think perhaps you should come back with me to Thornton Grange,' Jake decreed as they waited for their main course.

'Good heavens, why?' she asked,

stunned. 'Is anything wrong?'

'Calm down. Nothing's wrong. You look as if you could do with a break, that's all. You won't want to look a wreck on the wedding photos, will you?'

'Oh,' was all she could think to say.

'From what I saw this morning, I think it would be best if you took a couple of weeks off and spent some time with your parents.'

'What do you mean, what you saw this morning?' she snapped.

'You fraternising with the workmen, distracting them from their jobs. They're getting paid to work, not fool around.'

'They've all been working jolly hard, and I have not been fraternising with them as you so quaintly put it. I was giving Andy a hand when he needed it, that's all, otherwise he would have asked one of the other men. It was only for five minutes, for heaven's sake, nothing to get hysterical about.'

'For your information, I don't get hysterical.' His face was getting more thunderous by the minute.

'Anyway, who's going to look after things at Bay View if I'm not there?'

'The architect can earn his fee by doing that,' was his terse reply. 'He's getting paid plenty. Now, are you coming back with me tonight?'

'Well, if you're sure it will be all right.' She could tell that she had annoyed him, and after giving it some thought she realised how it must have looked when he arrived — Andy and her in the shower fully clothed, laughing riotously. 'I'd like to see your hotel where I'll be working eventually, and it would be nice to see more of my folks before they leave. No problem about a vacancy then?'

'I'm sure we can squeeze you in somewhere.' His mouth barely twitched at her attempt at a joke.

Nigel was inspecting Jake's car as they exited the restaurant. He seemed impressed, and when he saw Lexie he smiled, obviously their contretemps forgotten. 'Nice car,' he remarked.

'Don't suppose you're interested in parting company with it, are you, sir?'

Lexie had no choice but to perform the introductions. Jake and Nigel exchanged a few words about the car as Lexie settled in the passenger seat, and she sat comparing them as they discussed the Jaguar's vital statistics. It was a super car, but she couldn't understand how they could spend so much time talking about its top speed and what it did to the gallon, especially when they had just met.

Once they were underway, Jake remarked casually, 'Boyfriend?'

'No, just a friend,' she muttered. 'We've known each other since school days. We play badminton together.'

By the time they had made all the necessary arrangements and Lexie had packed, it was early evening. The church clock was striking seven as Jake nosed the car out of the Bay View car park. Its sumptuous leather interior enveloped her like a caress, so Lexie settled back to enjoy the ride despite

Jake's proximity. It was sheer unadulterated luxury, so superbly warm and comfortable; and since he was insisting she had a break, who was she to argue? It had been quite some time since she last had a holiday, and his hotel sounded so magnificent she was prepared to accept his offer and enjoy herself. No doubt when she joined his staff it would be a different kettle of fish, but she wasn't going to think about that right now.

She watched with respectful admiration as he manipulated his way effortlessly through the stream of traffic heading west. She guessed there must be a football match or something on because the roads was surprisingly busy. It gave her the opportunity to surreptitiously observe him more closely, since his attention was focused on the road ahead. His face, illuminated by the glow from the dashboard lights, was definitely handsome, especially when relaxed as it was now. Dark probing eyes, long aquiline nose and full sensuous lips. *I wonder what it would be like being kissed by them . . . held in those strong arms . . . have him murmur sweet nothings.* She wouldn't have shied away as she had with Nigel. Goodness, where were her thoughts taking her? Better think about all the other women who had occupied that passenger seat. Polly, for instance. She had called him several times while he was at Bay View. Was she special or just one of many female companions?

'Penny for your thoughts. Your eyes were gleaming like my cat's.'

'They're not worth even a penny,' she responded lightly, surprised he had noticed her appraisal. Did he have eyes in the back of his head, she wondered, or was it extra-sensory perception he practised?

'We'll stop for a bite to eat at the next service station, OK?'

'Fine,' she agreed readily enough, determined to try and keep the peace for as long as possible. 'I wouldn't mind a cup of tea. I seem to have drunk gallons with the builders around, what with the dust and all.'

'One gallon of tea coming up.' He sounded quite jaunty, and they swept into the outside lane and the car surged forward. A few miles further on, they pulled into a motorway café. They made it a quick stop since neither was particularly hungry and Lexie wasn't in a particularly chatty mood. The traffic had eased off by the time they rejoined, and Jake settled down to a more leisurely pace. 'We're going to be late back,' he told her. 'So if you feel like nodding off, feel free. The seat does recline.'

'Oh, I'm not tired in the least, thanks all the same.' She doubted if she could even doze with him so near. One had to be on the ball all the time he was around, and she didn't want him to think that she couldn't cope. After all, he must be tired since he had already made the trip once that day. However, before long her eyelids closed despite determined attempts to remain awake. The warmth and cosy atmosphere inside the car made her so drowsy she couldn't fight it any longer.

'Wake up, sleeping beauty. We've arrived.'

Lexie woke with a start. The car was pulling into a reserved parking place outside a dimly lit building. She blinked self-consciously. 'Sorry, I didn't mean to sleep.'

'At least you didn't snore.'

Lexie pulled herself together and after several attempts managed to open the car door and extricate herself. She couldn't see much of the hotel as it was mostly in darkness, but a light still shone from the entrance porch illuminating part of the driveway. It was after midnight and all was quiet. Jake retrieved her suitcase and let them in at the front door with his own set of keys. He then led Lexie up some stairs and along a corridor to a door at the end.

'Since this will be your room when you're on the staff, I thought you might like to get the feel of it,' he said, placing her case on a stand at the bottom of the bed. 'Sleep well. I'll see you in the morning. Good night, Lexie.'

She was now fully awake and wandered round the room, running her fingers along the single bed with its attractive floral duvet, matching curtains and bedside lampshade. She opened a door and found an ensuite toilet, wash basin and shower unit all in pastel pink. Such luxury — she didn't have to share with anyone else. Finally she unearthed her night clothes and had a quick shower; then feeling pleasantly relaxed, slipped into bed.

★  ★  ★

A loud knocking on the bedroom door woke her. Feeling somewhat disorientated, as if her brain had been scrambled, Lexie mumbled 'Just a minute' before hurriedly dragging on her dressing gown.

'Good morning — I'm Polly. I believe

we've spoken on the phone? Jake — I mean Mr Thornton — said to bring you this.' The young woman, about her own age, handed Lexie a breakfast tray. She looked bright and fresh, with a mischievous glint in her eye. 'He thought you might appreciate breakfast in your room just this once.'

'Good morning,' Lexie muttered, pulling her dressing-gown cord tightly round her and feeling at a distinct disadvantage. She hadn't had time to even brush her hair, and sensed Polly taking a full inventory. She probably concluded Lexie was no rival for Jake's favours — no threat to her. 'Thanks. I must have overslept.'

'Mr Thornton said to tell you he'll come for you in half an hour to take you to your parents' suite.'

★   ★   ★

For the next couple of weeks, Lexie thoroughly enjoyed being spoilt by her new-found father. They went for long walks whenever the weather was appropriate and participated in the sports facilities provided at the hotel. Alex proved to be an excellent swimmer and tried to teach her how to dive. Her mother seemed content to be a spectator, clearly delighted to see Lexie and Alex hitting it off so well. Lexie thought if she had to leave Ravenstone she couldn't think of a nicer place to come and work for a living. The scenery was quite breathtaking, the autumnal colours incredible. It was an artist's paradise.

★ ★ ★

The wedding took place at the tiny church in the next village, followed by a reception at Thornton Grange. The sun managed to break through, tinting the bracken and shrubs along the route and making a fairy-tale scene, breathtakingly beautiful. It was the first wedding Lexie had attended, and she enjoyed every minute, feeling immense pride as

96

her parents took their vows. She glanced across at Jake, wondering what his thoughts were at that precise moment. Did the solemnity of the occasion make him feel at all inspired to follow suit? Did he ever envisage getting married, or was he a confirmed bachelor convinced all females were out to trap him? She could imagine many women would think him a worthy challenge in the matrimonial stakes.

After the charmingly simple ceremony, Jake drove Lexie back to Thornton Grange. She felt a strange excitement. Her mother was now a married woman — something that took some reconciling. What would it be like going on honeymoon, sharing a bed with a man? She glanced at Jake and blushed. The thought of sharing a bed with him was petrifying.

'It's a remarkably picturesque part of the country,' she remarked. She had to say something to break the silence in case he could read her thoughts. 'I've never seen such wonderful scenery. And

97

look at that waterfall — how marvellous.'

'I hope you'll come to love it as much as Ravenstone,' Jake said, keeping his eyes on the road ahead. He looked most impressive in his dark wedding suit, she thought, but he did not smile. He had remained somewhat aloof throughout, although he had completed his duties meticulously as she had come to expect. Now he appeared preoccupied, perhaps contemplating the arrangements for the reception and wondering if all was in place.

Lexie sighed. 'That reminds me. I'll have to be getting back home now my holiday is over, but I have no transport. I wonder if Alex will lend me his car, since he won't need it for the next month or so?'

He frowned. 'Alex is driving to the airport, don't forget. Their choice. I did offer to be their chauffeur. Besides, there's no hurry about your return to Bay View. In fact, I think it would be a good idea if you started work here now instead of in the New Year.'

Lexie looked at him in amazement. He'd sounded so . . . so dictatorial. 'But I must go home and finish off the flat. I left in rather a hurry, if you remember. My room is only half done — I need some more clothes.' Lexie, startled by his announcement, floundered uncomfortably. It wasn't just because he wanted her to stay, but the way he intimated he had decided and would brook no argument. There was no negotiation. He decreed she should remain and that was the end of the matter.

'When necessary, I will drive you over to Ravenstone,' he continued, seemingly unaware of the turmoil he had caused. 'For the moment, you'll be better occupied here, and as for clothes, you'll be wearing the hotel uniform most of the time.'

Lexie stared at his changed manner — so coldly officious. 'But . . . '

'I want you to start work at the reception desk first thing Monday morning. You'll be able to relieve Polly. We're going to be short-handed otherwise. The sooner you learn how we operate and get to grips with our system, the better.'

There didn't seem to be anything she could say. He was demonstrating quite clearly he was the boss and she would have to toe the line. She'd already got the impression he was a chameleon, and yet it was only with her he seemed so stern and forbidding. During the last two weeks, whenever others were present, he was perfectly charming and conciliatory; but on the odd occasion they'd been alone, his attitude had been quite different. She had thought maybe she was imagining it, but now she knew she hadn't. He really didn't like her! He was making it plainly obvious.

Lexie remained silent for the rest of the journey. She didn't want to upset her parents on such a happy occasion, but inside she was fuming. Back at the hotel she ignored Jake as best she could, and fortunately since the bridal pair had a plane to catch, the reception wasn't prolonged. She remembered little of it, however, being too wrapped up in her own private misery. Was this typical of how it was going to be in future? What had she done to deserve such censure? Should she demand an explanation? What would be the use? She had agreed to work for him, hadn't she?

After the newlyweds' departure, Lexie managed to escape to her room, where she flopped on the bed to evaluate her position. With her parents now happily married and unaware of what she'd agreed to, somehow or other she had to put up with Jake until she had repaid him in full, but she knew it was going to be far more difficult than she had ever anticipated. Her only hope was that the flats sold quickly, thereby relieving her of any commitment to him. Once he had been repaid, she could return to Ravenstone or any-where else that took her fancy.

A maid arrived and handed her a

parcel. It contained her uniform. She threw it on the chair in a fit of pique. How could he! The wedding was hardly over, and here he was reminding her again of her duty. Had he no sensitivity! Feeling totally bereft, she slipped out of her wedding finery, donned a warm jumper and jeans, and headed for the door. She had to escape for a while. Emerging from the lift, it was her luck to bump into Jake coming from his office.

'Lifts are out of bounds to members of staff remember,' he muttered darkly, striding purposefully towards the lounge. Lexie was hopping mad. If she had transport, she would have left and returned to Ravenstone regardless of what Jake Thornton decreed. He didn't own her. By the time she got her temper under some sort of control, she had tramped quite a distance up the road, and seeing a path leading off round the back of the lake, she took it. Gradually the beauty of the scenery took over and she calmed down, though she was still cursing the day she had met the aggressive, insensitive, hateful bully of a step-brother, Jake Thornton.

'Hello. You're from the hotel up the road, aren't you?'

'Yes. Have we met?' She frowned. He looked a personable young man, fresh-faced with short fair hair and teasing blue eyes.

'Not officially been introduced, but I saw you there last week. I'm the local doctor, and I gather you're coming to work here. I like to know about any new prospective patients — especially the attractive ones.' He flashed her a whimsical smile.

'Lexie Prescott,' she introduced her-self, gratified by his manner. It was balm to her frayed nerves.

'Delighted to meet you, Lexie. I'm Simon Jackson. Mind if I join you?'

'Not at all. Since I'm new around here, I could do with a guide; but weren't you heading in the opposite direction?'

'We can't have you getting lost now, can we? In any case, I could do with the exercise. It's such a beautiful day. At this time of year, one has to make the most of them.'

Simon told her something about the area and places to go for walks and helped her negotiate some stepping stones through a muddy patch. He even tentatively arranged to take her up one of the hills some day, although he admitted he could never guarantee something wouldn't come up at the last minute and he'd have to call it off.

'That's all right. I don't know what my duty times are yet,' Lexie said, grimacing slightly. 'I've just been told I'm to start work here now rather than after New Year. It was unwelcome news. I had things to do back in Ravenstone.'

'Boyfriend waiting for you?' He grinned.

'No. No boyfriend just things to do.'

They arrived back at the hotel, where they parted company. 'I look forward to seeing you around, Lexie Prescott. I'm sure you'll like it here when you settle in.' And with a cheery wave, he jauntily strode off down to the village.

★   ★   ★

Monday morning Lexie was getting ready for work when someone knocked on the door. Calling 'Come in!' from the bathroom, she finished putting on her make-up before going to see who it was. She was taken aback to find Jake sitting on her bed. 'Sorry, I thought it was the maid,' she muttered.

'How's the uniform?' His eyes clinically swept her from top to toe.

'As you can see, it fits.' Conscious of his studied approval, she glowered at him.

'I came to give you some last-minute reminders since you're now a fully fledged member of staff. I expect courtesy and civility at all times. Visitors like to see smiling faces, so no matter how difficult and trying they may be, I expect you to keep your temper. The facilities are for the visitors, and can only be used by members of staff at the appropriate times listed on the noticeboard in the staff quarters. Is that clear?'

'Yes,' she said through gritted teeth. He wasn't telling her anything she didn't already know.

'I can't make any exceptions to the rules, Lexie. Even I stick by them.'

'I don't expect preferential treatment, so if you don't mind, I have to be on duty in ten minutes and I have to finish getting ready. Was there anything else you wished to instruct me on?' She glanced at her watch rather pointedly.

'No, not for the moment. I hope you'll be happy working here.' He got up to leave. 'I think you'll find it quite different from Bay View. It should be somewhat easier once you've mastered your duties, and you'll be paid the going rate for the job like anyone else, since you don't want preferential treatment,' was his parting shot.

When he had gone, Lexie threw a

cushion at the bed to relieve her pent-up anger. She made a pact with herself that she would appear composed and do her job as efficiently as possible, but would keep out of Jake's way. She was going to make certain he never had anything to complain about. She ought to have known his proposal of help was too good to be true. Oh, she knew he had saved them financially, but need he be so bossy? She checked herself over in the wardrobe mirror, grimacing at the uniform. If she were truthful, though, she knew it was smart — royal-blue blazer, white blouse and white pleated skirt, with white slacks for the male members. It made the staff look part of a team and yet did not detract from the informality that pervaded the hotel.

Promptly at eight o'clock, she reported to the reception desk where Polly was to show her the ropes. Despite her earlier reservations, Polly proved to be very easy to get along with. She looked younger than Lexie had expected and not the sophisticated woman she anticipated Jake to date, but there was no doubt about her friendliness. She showed Lexie where everything was in the office and talked her through the procedures done daily with no sign of animosity. In fact, she seemed genuinely pleased to see her. Since Lexie had not worked a computer booking system before, she found it very confusing and complicated and felt a complete novice. It was all so different from Bay View. By the end of her shift, she was totally bewildered by the new technology and expertise which Polly took so much for granted, making it look like child's play.

'Coming for lunch?' Polly asked. 'I'm famished. I wonder what's on the menu today? I haven't had time to look. I hear Jake's your step-brother,' Polly said, plonking her bag down on a chair. 'I think he's rather dishy, don't you? Everybody here thinks so — at least all the women do,' she added with a chuckle.

Lexie could think of several adjectives she would use to describe him, but let it pass and asked how long she thought it would take to train her to do the job. Obviously Polly didn't feel altogether secure in her relationship with Jake, but was putting on a brave face.

'Oh, you'll soon get the hang of it,' Polly said with a grin. 'After all, if I can do it, I'm jolly sure you can. I left school with hardly any qualifications. The main object is to keep the guests happy at all costs.'

Polly was infectiously friendly, and Lexie could see why Jake would find her attractive. She had Lexie laughing at some of the guests' antics she had observed, and had a delightful sense of humour. She might be young, but she had a confidence about her and the knack of putting people at their ease, which was of paramount importance.

After lunch, Lexie had some free time before going on duty again. It was decidedly cold and breezy out, and yet she didn't feel like staying in her room. Since the pool was out of bounds, she decided to brave the elements to go for a walk. She headed towards the village, walking briskly in order to keep warm. She met a few hikers with packs on their backs who greeted her in a friendly fashion, and when she reached the village shop she went in to buy some postcards and stamps. Next door was a store selling hiking equipment which Alex had been trying to interest her in buying. She looked at the boots and anoraks in the window thoughtfully, wondering if it was going to be worth her while buying any. Would she be at Thornton Grange long enough? Deciding to leave it for a while longer, she set off back again.

On the way, she made up her mind to speak to Jake and find out exactly how long she would have to work until he deemed the debt paid. She had to know how long it would be before she was free to seek employment elsewhere. He had steamrollered her into a hasty decision. At the time, she thought it would be interesting working alongside him more as a partner and an equal. Now she realised that was not what he intended at all. She could not understand the change in him and wondered what she had done to cause it. She trekked back, mulling over what he had said and realised she must have misinterpreted some of it somewhere along the line. She knew she hadn't been thinking clearly at the time. She wished she was back in Ravenstone; at least there she was her own boss, even if she was a prisoner after dark. She wasn't sure what to do about her wages, as she hadn't expected to be paid any.

'Going my way?' Simon Jackson pulled up alongside, offering her a lift.

'Thanks, if you're going by Thornton Grange. It's much colder out than I thought,' she said, scrambling into the passenger seat gratefully.

'I was heading there anyway. Trouble at the mill, as they say.'

'Oh dear, I hope it isn't anything

serious,' Lexie replied with due concern.

'I doubt it. I mostly get called out there when someone unaccustomed to exercise oversteps the limit. They think they can catch up in two weeks what they couldn't do in the other fifty,' he remarked dryly. 'Some people never learn!'

He didn't hang about though, and they were soon entering the hotel grounds. They both hurried into the entrance, where Jake met Simon with the news the patient was in the pool changing room.

\* \* \*

During the following week, Lexie could feel Jake watching her, waiting to find fault, to pounce on any mistake no matter how trivial. By the time she went to bed at night, she was a nervous wreck and so keyed up trying to do everything perfectly she couldn't sleep. It was a nightmare because she was so fearful of doing something wrong. Thornton Grange was nothing like Bay View. Here everything was modern and technical; the hotel seemed to run smoothly and efficiently as if on oiled wheels, with everyone doing their job happily and easily except herself. She struggled to memorise the names of local towns, the bus timetable and the steamer sailing times. Then there was the computerised accounting to come to terms with, and an electric type-writer instead of her old-fashioned manual one. The guests were much more friendly and pleasant than she'd had to cope with at Bay View though, and she found herself having to fend off amorous young men quite often. That gave her a fillip — a badly needed fillip.

During her off-duty hours, she mentally made notes of what she had learned, wholly determined Jake would not have any reason to complain about her work. Polly was a good teacher, thankfully, and didn't make her feel too foolish when she asked for help, particularly making out the clients' accounts — she would hate to get those wrong. She was jealous of Polly's casual friendliness with Jake. She often saw them laughing together and wished Jake would be like that with her, but if anything he seemed stricter than ever. By the time it was her day off, she was more than ready for it, and took herself for a walk to blow the cobwebs away despite it being rather cold and damp. As each day passed, she became a little more confident, and was even starting to enjoy the work — at least she would if it had not been for Jake. He seemed to haunt her even in her dreams.

Gradually she got used to the regime, and the rest of the staff proved to be friendly to work with. At Bay View she had been on call more or less all day every day, and now it seemed strange having so much time off — time to read books she hadn't found time for before, and pleasant having other young people to talk to in the staffroom. She had even taken up knitting again, something she used to do but hadn't done for such a long time. Life was so very different! The scenery she found exceedingly beautiful, and finally she bought some walking boots and waterproof clothing so she could explore it. The weather was unpredictable, and after having got caught out in the not infrequent heavy showers once too often, she decided to be prepared at all times as the brochures and guide books suggested. She saw Simon occasionally when she went down to the village, and sometimes he called in for a quiet drink at the bar. He always made a great display of pleasure at seeing her, which lifted her morale no end. He was a likeable guy and she enjoyed his easy banter.

On her day off one week, she took the bus into Windermere to do some shopping and have a general browse around. She bought some Christmas presents and cards, then treated herself to lunch at a small café before boarding the bus back. The feeling of having free time all to herself was marvellous, so the next week she decided to go to Keswick, where her parents had taken her previously. She liked the town nestling in the valley with its ring of mountains for protection. Its cobbled market place intrigued her, as did the little arcade shops and boutiques which even at this time of the year proved to be busy and thriving. She finished her shopping, then went for a coffee; and as she emerged from the café, she practically bumped into Simon, who was passing.

'Good heavens, what a surprise! Fancy meeting you here,' he said cheerfully.

'We'll have to stop meeting like this,' she teased. 'People will start to talk.'

He grinned. 'Are you staying in Keswick long?'

'No. I'm filling in time until the bus comes. I haven't brought my own car over yet from Ravenstone, so I'm reduced to catching public transport.'

'Well, if you don't mind waiting, I'll gladly give you a lift back. I've got one more port of call.'

'If you're sure you don't mind a passenger, I'd be grateful.'

'Meet me in the car park over there in, say, a quarter of an hour?'

'Lovely. I'll have time to call in that marvellous book shop I saw round the corner.'

On the way back, Simon kept up a lively conversation, making Lexie laugh gaily, and she replied with equally witty remarks. He had a way of bringing out her youthful spirit that the cares and worries of Bay View had dampened, and she arrived back at the hotel in a happy frame of mind.

'You look as if you've enjoyed your day off,' remarked Debbie when she entered the reception area.

'Oh, I have. I've been to Keswick, and Doctor Jackson gave me a lift back.'

'He's nice, isn't he?'

'Yes, he's great fun,' Lexie replied, quickly making for the stairs when she saw Jake heading in their direction.

'Lexie,' he called out after her, 'might I have a word?' He sounded reasonably amicable for a change.

'Sure. Something I can do?'

'I've been thinking over your suggestions for other amenities. I'm not sure if horse riding or pony trekking would be a good idea — not in the short term, at any rate. But I like the scheme you had about organised guided walks and minibus outings. They could be accomplished as a joint venture. Some walkers like to be dropped off at a distance from the hotel and make their own way back, while other guests only come for the scenery and can't walk far.'

'Yes, that's what I thought.'

'We'll have to see if we can lay our hands on suitable transport, but other things being equal, I believe we should go ahead and try it. Well done!'

As he turned away, she added, 'It was something Simon said that gave me the idea.'

Jake's eyebrows rose and he shrugged his shoulders, clearly not pleased by her latest piece of information, and she wished she'd left it unsaid.

# 6

Simon installed her in the passenger seat of his small saloon car with exaggerated politeness. 'May I say how smashing you look? I expect you've suitors by the score. I'm gratified that you deign to accompany me on your day off. Where would you like to go, fair maiden?'

'I don't know this area, remember, so surprise me,' she laughed.

'So be it, milady. One mystery tour coming up. Fasten your seat belt, here we go.'

Lexie resolved to forget Jake; to forget Bay View and even Thornton Grange for the whole day. She wanted to shut out all her problems for a few hours, and Simon proved to be an ideal companion, so it was easier than she had imagined. It was a wonderful day. The sun shone briefly through breaks in the clouds as they drove through narrow twisting country lanes and small idyllic villages. The scenery was awesome, especially when they motored up to a high pass on a road full of tight hairpin bends with a steep drop at the side. Lexie clung nervously to the seat as Simon negotiated each turn, and she was extremely thankful when they reached the top in one piece.

He grinned at her. 'I must have been up here a thousand times and haven't spun off yet. Never fear; I know this area like the back of my hand.'

'It's great,' she called back, and her stomach lurched when they hit a hump in the road. The next minute she was hurtling towards the windscreen, but restrained by her seat belt as he quickly jabbed on the brakes to avoid a sheep which had decided at the last minute to join its companions on the other side of the road.

'Nearly had lamb stew for lunch,' he joked, completely unfazed.

'It appeared to be glaring at you rather indignantly and had such a snooty look on its face,' she laughed nervously. 'I suppose they do have the right of way around here.'

They stopped for lunch at a roadside pub, where Simon had her in stitches telling her riotous stories of his exploits at medical school before, as he said, 'settling down to life as a modest GP' in his home village. He had taken over his father's practice, and his father stood in for him so he could have a day off now and then. It sounded a very pleasant arrangement. 'You really ought to join some of the activities in the village. It may surprise you what goes on here. We put on plays and slide shows, have jumble sales and all sorts of things for fund raising — mainly for the proverbial church roof.'

'Do you take part in the plays?' she asked with genuine amusement.

'Oh yes. I'm the leading light around here, I'll have you know.' He said it with such a straight face that Lexie wondered if it was true. He had such a dry sense of humour at times.

'I'll certainly make the attempt if I'm here long enough,' she promised.

'What! You're not thinking of leaving us already, surely? You've just got here. I'll have to speak to Jake about that. We can't lose you so soon.'

'I was only joking,' she said, anxious Simon didn't say anything to Jake until she had a chance to talk to him. She had kept putting it off, but one way or another she would have to steel herself into doing so. In the afternoon they had a delightful ramble round some small tarns before the light faded and it was time to motor back.

Simon opened the car door and helped her out in the car park with deferential decorum, asking if she would like to repeat the prescription again sometime.

'I'd like that very much, Simon. I enjoyed today immensely. The area has much to commend it, for sure. I'll even go so far as to say it compares favourably with Ravenstone where I come from.'

He left with a wave, and she walked indoors feeling on top of the world.

* * *

Jake had seen Lexie leaving the hotel that morning, and the look on her face as she greeted Jackson had got under his skin. She appeared thrilled to see him. He heard her chuckle at Jackson's banter, which irritated him beyond belief. He ought to be pleased she had found someone to befriend her, to take her out and show her something of the countryside; but for some unknown reason he was annoyed. All day he couldn't think about anything else but Lexie, wondering what they were up to. He had told Alex he would keep an eye on his daughter, but she was old enough to go out on dates and certainly didn't need his permission. He watched from his office window as the afternoon wore on, and heaved a sigh when the car cruised into the car park and drew up outside the front door. At least they were in one piece, but he didn't care for Jackson's style of driving — too fast in his opinion, especially for a doctor. Without thinking twice, he went out into the reception area and waited for Lexie.

She breezed through the front door still smiling, her face a picture of health and happiness.

'I'd like to see you in my office — now,' Jake growled as soon as she stepped through the door, pulling her back to earth with a bump.

'Now what have I done?' she sighed. Pulling off her anorak, she followed him into his private domain. Trust him to put a damper on things and spoil her day.

'I take it you've been out with Jackson all day?' he barked.

'What's wrong with that? It was my day off,' she said defensively.

'I don't like you getting so friendly

with any Tom, Dick or Harry when you've hardly been here five minutes.'

'What on earth has it to do with you who I'm friendly with? He's not a hotel guest and you are not my keeper, Jake. If I choose to go out with Simon or anybody else, then I shall do so. By the way, while I'm here I'd like to know how I stand with regard to our financial arrangement. How long do you intend keeping me here to pay off the debt?'

'Want to run out on it already?' he gibed.

'I'd like to know so I can look for another job in plenty of time, that's all,' she replied, tilting her head defiantly and managing to hold his gaze.

'Do you need reminding of your precarious state of affairs?' After a significant pause which made her lower her eyes and fume inwardly, he added, 'As for how long, I should think at least until the flats are complete and ready for sale. That would seem fair, wouldn't you think?'

'But . . . I can't be in two places at

once, and while I'm here I don't know what's going on at Bay View.' She turned to leave with a deep sigh of regret. 'I don't know why I ever went along with your scheme in the first place. You've manipulated me all along. I thought I was going to be more of a partner here, not merely another member of staff.'

'I didn't ask you in here to discuss your leaving. I'd like to make a deal with you.'

'I'd rather make a deal with the devil,' she muttered half under her breath, but paused with her hand on the door handle, compelled to hear him out.

'For personal reasons, Lexie, I'd like your co-operation in a subterfuge.' Propping himself up against the desk, he looked every inch the man in charge of her destiny. 'I need someone to act as my fiancée, and I want you to be that person. What do you say?'

'I beg your pardon? I don't believe what I'm hearing.' She stared at him in stunned disbelief. 'You want me to pretend to be your fiancée? Why on earth should I do such a ridiculous thing?'

Jake pondered for a moment before replying, 'Maybe so I'll keep paying the bills to transform your old home into something you can be proud of. Is that a good enough reason?' He knew it sounded weak, but it was the best he could come up with.

'And if I don't? You can't very well fire me.' She looked up with a gleam of hope in her eyes. 'You can't back out of our deal?'

'No, but I could make life very uncomfortable for you. Dammit, Lexie, would it be such an onerous task to pretend a loving relationship with me? It's not a lot to ask. After all, we're almost related.'

Lexie was thinking desperately, trying to work out what he was up to this time. He always seemed so plausible. What possible motive could he have? 'Who are you trying to fool with this pretence? Polly?' she asked, knowing when she was beaten and did not wish to give him the pleasure of an argument, which he would win as usual. She felt rather sorry for Polly, though, and couldn't think why he wanted to be so devious.

'Good heavens, what's Polly got to do with it? She's leaving soon to get married. That's why you were required here in the first place. And I still haven't found a replacement for the under-manger. I've got enough on my plate.'

'Oh, I didn't know. I thought . . . Well, then who?'

'Never mind who or why,' he said coldly. 'That's neither here nor there. Do I take it you agree? It's only a temporary measure, I assure you.'

'I suppose so. I don't seem to have much option, do I? I'd like it in writing that on completion of the flats, I'm free to leave and find other employment. This isn't what I expected when I agreed to your proposition.'

'You have my word; but if that isn't good enough, I'll put it in writing. I'll even give you a reference. How does that sound? Now, I propose we go out to dinner tomorrow to celebrate our engagement. We may as well set the ball rolling straight away.'

'You realise I haven't anything suitable to wear, and I should be working tomorrow evening,' she said stubbornly. She knew she could wear her wedding outfit for such an occasion, but didn't feel obliged to mention it. She was determined not to make things any easier for him.

'That's no problem; you may have tomorrow off. As it happens, I have to go to Kendal on business, so you could do some shopping at the same time. I'll need to be away by half past nine, so if you want a lift, be down by then.'

Dismissed, Lexie found herself walking up to her room in a daze. Why on earth had she been talked into such a stupid scheme? He had done it again. He had managed to bewilder her into doing something totally against her better judgement. How did he manage it?

Lexie hardly slept a wink. The next morning she was up early, wondering if perhaps she had been dreaming. Had she really agreed to act as Jake's fiancée? She must want her head examining. She shook it in bewilderment when she remembered the proposed visit to Kendal; it had been no dream, more like a nightmare!

She turned the shower on full and let the warm cascading water reawaken her senses as she tried to unravel her chaotic thoughts. Jake could have any number of women queuing up happy to act as his fiancée, so why had he chosen her? Then she realised they would all want to hold him to the commitment and expect to marry him, and he obviously wanted to keep them at bay by pretending he already had a girlfriend. That made sense! He didn't want to be pinned down by anyone female — why should he, when he could change them as often as he changed his socks?

Wrapped in a towel, she pottered about the bedroom wondering who he wanted to deceive if it wasn't Polly. She hadn't seen any other female around who could account for it. Seeing the mist on the mountain tops and pockets of snow in the crevices, she dressed in a thick woollen jumper and skirt, then collecting her anorak she went down to breakfast.

Polly greeted her in the staffroom and asked her conspiratorially how she'd managed to wangle the day off. 'Preferential treatment?' she mocked.

'I don't know about that,' said Lexie, not able to meet her friend's eyes, 'but I have to go to Kendal today on a family matter and Jake said he'd give me a lift.'

'I was only joking. Actually, Jake is usually co-operative if you need time off, provided you can give him a good enough reason of course. Anyway, I can do with all the extra overtime I can get at the moment; I'm saving for my bottom drawer. Not long now before I take the plunge.'

'Who's the lucky guy?' Lexie asked. 'Not someone local by any chance?'

'No such luck. I fell for a sailor based in Portsmouth of all places. I'm not sure how I'll take to living down there.'

★   ★   ★

'I'm glad to see you're punctual,' Jake remarked, opening the car door for Lexie. He obviously had not changed his mind. It was the first time since the wedding day she had been alone in such close proximity to him, and she could feel his masculinity overwhelming her again. No other man had ever had this effect on her, so what was it about Jake that made him different? she wondered. She was friendly with most of the male members of staff and quite at ease in their company, but somehow Jake made her feel like an adolescent teenager.

She huddled in the passenger seat,

watching as he drove along the winding lane. He had large well-shaped hands with exceptionally long fingers which were now curved lightly round the steering wheel, almost caressing the car along. How decisive and self-assured he looked, even casually dressed as he was today. If anything, the high-necked sweater and cord trousers accentuated his autocratic image. Why hadn't she refused to co-operate in this silly pretence? What had got into her? She used to be so serene in a crisis, able to cope with anything, but now she was a nervous wreck whenever he was around. Silently she tried to summon up some of her old self-control and poise. She was coping all right with the job; there had been no complaints as far as she knew. She should feel justifiably proud at how well she had adapted to the new regime in such a short time. Polly had said she she'd taken to it like a duck to water.

Sitting up, she straightened her shoulders and began taking notice of the passing scenery, refusing to be cowed by him. After all, she was only twenty years old. She would have liked to have asked Jake about his motives for the charade but decided not to. She would more than likely have had the same answer — it was none of her business. *I won't let him get to me*, she thought. *I won't. I won't.*

They came over the brow of the hill and saw Kendal spread out in the valley below. It was an overcast day with smoke rising from the chimneys of the cottages at the roadside. She thought they looked rather pleasant despite the gloomy weather. Built of local grey stone with grey-green slate roofs, they were quite distinctive — cosy-looking.

'I'll be about two hours. Will that be long enough for your requirements?' Jake broke the silence that had lasted throughout the journey.

'I expect it will be fine,' she replied indifferently.

Pulling into a bay of the multi-storey car park, Jake switched off the engine.

His expression was grim. 'Think you can manage a more friendly attitude?'

She gulped. 'I . . . I didn't think we'd . . . '

He gave a deep sigh, extracted some money from his wallet and gave it to her. 'I think that should cover it.'

'What do you mean? I don't want your money.' Angrily she thrust it back at him. 'I am quite capable of buying my own clothes, thank you very much. I'm not quite destitute.' She scrambled out of the car and heard him call after her to meet him back there at twelve o' clock.

Lexie had no idea where she would find the sort of shop she was looking for, never having been to Kendal before, and was extremely anxious about the cost of a suitable outfit despite her show of bravado. She tried to recall pictures she had seen in the magazines, but her mind was a blank. She had been told many times green was her colour to match her eyes, but the style was what concerned her more.

Dress or two-piece? Long or short? Long sleeves or bare-shouldered? She pulled a face at her reflection in a shop window. She had never even tried on one of those exotic evening creations.

As luck would have it, she happened to pass a small boutique in a side street soon after leaving the car park. In the window were some reasonably priced cocktail dresses. Two elegant women entered the shop, so she decided to follow them. The assistant would be busy serving them, which would give her time to browse first. It turned out to be a much larger establishment than it first appeared, and Lexie wandered round seeking inspiration. It was a bewildering choice, and she felt out of her depth.

Eventually an assistant accosted her. 'Can I be of assistance? Are you looking for anything special?'

'I really don't know what I'm looking for,' Lexie said with a desperate sigh. 'I could do with something elegant yet practical. I have a special date tonight.'

The assistant began sliding dresses along the racks and pulled out one or two which she thought might be appropriate. 'I'm sure with your figure we should be able to find something suitable,' she remarked with a friendly smile.

Lexie became more and more bewildered. None of the dresses seemed quite what she had in mind, yet time was going and she had to buy something. As she was about to leave and try her luck somewhere else, the assistant said to wait a minute and disappeared into the rear of the shop. She returned shortly after with a shantung silk dress and jacket in a most attractive shade of green, somewhere between sea green and turquoise. Lexie fell in love with it the minute she set eyes on it.

'Do try it on. I'm sure it will suit you admirably,' the assistant urged. 'It's just arrived, straight from London. We kept it back for one of our usual clients, but

I'm sure it will suit you down to the ground.'

Lexie stared at herself in the full-length mirror. The dress definitely did something for her. It was superbly cut and fitted like a glove, making her feel ever so sophisticated. She had never possessed such a dress, but knew instinctively it was what any girlfriend of Jake's would wear. That made her pause for a moment, but taking another look, she decided that despite the alarmingly high price tag, she would buy it and hang the expense. If necessary, she could dip into the wages she had put away untouched. She comforted herself it was for Jake's benefit, so in a way he should be paying for it.

She left the boutique feeling well pleased with her purchase and spent the rest of the time until twelve o' clock window shopping in the Westmorland Centre. It was pleasant dawdling round the arcade shops all attractively deco-rated for Christmas and to hear the carols being played, even if it was a little premature. Eventually she looked at her watch and found it was almost time she went to meet Jake. Quickly she retraced her steps to the car park and saw him waiting in the car, patiently reading some paperwork.

★  ★  ★

Lexie spent a long time getting ready, determined Jake wouldn't be able to find fault with her appearance, although she did wonder why she was making such an effort. She had spent the afternoon helping out at reception, even though Jake had told her she could have the day off. She hadn't wanted to spend hours agonising over the ordeal to come. When she slipped the dress over her head, she knew it was exactly right for the occasion and would give her some much-needed courage. It was sleeveless, with a fitted bodice, respectable neckline and softly draped skirt. She had a feeling of sensuous pride when she looked in the mirror. It showed off her slim figure beautifully. She was glad she had bought it despite having depleted her bank account substantially. It was definitely morale-boosting. She hadn't realised how much difference clothes made.

Her hair she managed to tame into submission with loose bouncy curls. She had thought to put it up in a more elegant style but decided against it. She felt happiest with it free and casual. She wasn't a naturally sophisticated person, so Jake would have to accept that. Since arriving at Thornton Grange, her face wasn't quite so thin; she had more colour and generally looked much more vibrant and youthful. If he wanted a mature fiancée, then he should have asked someone else, she thought, pulling a face at her reflection. Dabbing on her favourite perfume, she picked up the jacket and walked downstairs feeling nervous but rather excited too. She felt altogether a different person and wished her mother could see her.

'Wow. You look fantastic. You look a million dollars,' Polly declared immediately she caught sight of her. 'What's the special occasion? Whoever he is, I hope he's loaded.'

'Now that would be telling,' laughed Lexie, delighted by her friend's commendation.

'Don't do anything I wouldn't do,' Polly replied jauntily. 'Have a nice time though, and don't forget your front door key.'

Lexie knocked on the office door and waited until Jake bid her enter. He was on the telephone, so she went and stood by the window until he had finished his conversation, not before noticing his glance of approval however. She turned, clutching her bag, her fingers digging in until they hurt when she heard him replace the receiver. She felt as tense as a coiled spring waiting for his comments. His bold protracted appraisal made her lower her eyes to examine the carpet in order to recover some of the lost composure which his presence induced. He said nothing, but set about locking the desk. Retrieving his jacket from the back of the chair, he picked up the car keys, and she hastily made her way to the door feeling aggrieved. He'd not said a word. Still, what had she expected?

'I've booked a table at the Golden Last,' he said, switching off the light. He called goodnight to Polly. Polly's eyes glinted mischievously, and Lexie knew that by the time they reached the restaurant the news would have spread through the staff quarters like wildfire. She wondered what Polly would make of it, and knew she was in for a grilling when next they met. Getting into his sports car with its low-slung seats proved to be a difficult operation without displaying a considerable amount of leg. Lexie's skirt rode up embarrassingly. So much for elegance she thought, noticing the quirk of his lips as Jake closed the door. She shuffled to make herself decent, muttering under her breath, and wishing it was nice easy-going Simon taking her out.

The ride to the restaurant was mercifully short, so conversation wasn't necessary. Lexie stared straight ahead, feeling hot and flustered. Maybe the dress was a mistake. Perhaps it wasn't suitable for the Golden Last. Was Jake embarrassed by her choice of outfit? He swung the car through the narrow entrance to the restaurant car park and Lexie's eyes quickly surveyed the attractive old building. It didn't look too big, but maybe it was rather exclusive, she thought anxiously, fumbling with the door catch. *Pull yourself together*, she admonished herself, and quickly emerged from the car before Jake could assist her.

The owner-manager greeted them with what seemed like genuine warmth. 'It's a pleasure to have you dining with us again, Mr Thornton. I have your usual table ready.'

The usual table was one set into an alcove giving discreet privacy for its occupants, and was attractively decorated with a table lamp and a small Christmassy display. Only a few tables were occupied, and subdued taped music made for a tranquil ambience. A hovering waiter handed them elaborate menus which reminded Lexie of those at the Royal in Ravenstone. How long ago was that? It seemed like years. What a lot had happened in those few short weeks. She perused the folder with growing anxiety, wondering what to choose. Should she ask Jake to order for her? Was that usual, or should she plump for the anything and hope for the best?

'May I say how charming you look,' Jake said, sensing her trepidation. 'You have exquisite choice. That shade of green suits you. You look stunning.'

Her heart fluttered. She smiled nervously, wondering what he would say if she told him how devastatingly handsome he looked in his smart dark suit and pearl-grey shirt. When he smiled, his face lit up, making him look like a choirboy, all angelic and cherubic; but on the other side of the coin, she knew only too well he could be quite forbidding.

'You often look as if you find something amusing which isn't obvious to me. Would you care to share the joke?' He said it in a teasing way with a quirky lift of an eyebrow, which made his features all the more arresting.

'I'm sure you wouldn't find it funny.' Lexie quickly buried her head in the menu.

'Fiancées aren't supposed to have secrets,' he interposed calmly, reminding her of the reason for their being there.

'Oh, it was nothing,' she murmured. 'Just some difference I was observing between men and women and the way they accept compliments. What would you say if I acknowledged how smart you're looking tonight? You too have excellent taste.'

'I'd be extremely gratified you'd even noticed what I was wearing,' he answered suavely. 'Would you like some help with your choice from the menu? I can recommend the house speciality.'

She nodded, grateful she wouldn't be made to look incompetent.

When the waiter had taken their order, Jake produced a small red box from his pocket. 'I trust this meets with your approval?' Inside was a magnificent ring — a superb diamond surrounded by a cluster of emeralds. He slipped it on her finger without further ado before she realised what was happening. Lexie gazed at the ring with incredulity. Until that moment, she really hadn't thought too much about what she had agreed to do. It had all seemed so melodramatic that she hadn't taken it seriously. The feel of the ring brought it home to her how stupid it was to tolerate being party to the pretence. It was against all her principles, and yet she couldn't take her eyes off it. The stones sparkled in the subdued lighting. They mocked her — called her a traitor.

'It's very beautiful,' she whispered as icy fingers played havoc with her spine. How could she shiver when her face burned? She gulped and looked across at him. He was watching her with a curious expression on his face. For a moment their eyes were locked together, and she experienced sheer panic.

'How long . . . how long do you wish me to wear it?' Thankfully her voice sounded calm and controlled and didn't betray how she actually felt.

'I'm glad you like it,' he replied in a matter-of-fact tone as he shook out his serviette, completely ignoring her question.

The arrival of their first course interrupted the conversation, which gave her time to recover. She was making a discovery and the shock was devastating. Jake raised his glass to toast their engagement. Lexie managed a sip of champagne and knew without a doubt that if Jake really loved her, she would be the happiest woman alive.

That was why she had accepted the proposition without much of a fight! She wanted his respect — something she had yearned for since they first met; but most of all, she wanted his love. She was in love with him! But she was living in a fantasy world. Ever since their first meeting, she had been overcome by his charismatic personality. She ought to have seen it coming. Jake was the first person to ruffle her composure. She recalled the time they were introduced and how she had been thrown into turmoil from which she hadn't recovered. The sudden perception of her true feelings was mind-blowing. She had been seeking his approval ever since her arrival at Thornton Grange, and now she realised why. She must be mad to even consider it.

'You're not exactly looking enthusiastic,' he scolded her gently.

'I'm sorry,' she whispered. 'I don't like lies. I really don't know how you managed to talk me into this. It's crazy. It's not real.'

'What if it were for real?' he asked. 'Would that make so much difference?'

That caused her more panic. Had he read her thoughts? Could he do that too?

'When I get engaged . . . if I ever get engaged it will because I'm in love,' she half sobbed, stammering with misgivings. 'This isn't going to work. I'm not an actress. You'll have to find somebody else.' But she made no move to remove the ring. She liked the feel of it on her finger and yet at the same time was appalled by the travesty.

'Lexie, look at me.' He stroked her hand gently — calmly — soothingly. 'Come now, don't get upset. It will only be until after Christmas — New Year at the latest. Surely you can keep up an appearance of something like affection for me that long? Am I so abhorrent to you?'

'I don't find you abhorrent,' she burst out candidly. 'I don't like deceit, and what are my parents going to think when we call it off? Oh, it's useless. I shall have to explain everything to them. I'll see if I can find some other way to finance the building work. I should never have . . . ' She was again beginning to regret ever having met Jake Thornton. She wanted to run away and hide like an immature schoolgirl. She felt out of her depth. Her feelings see-sawed alarmingly. How was it possible to be in love with someone who disturbed her in such a way? At times she thought she hated him.

Jake sighed, removed his hand and began attacking his melon starter. 'There's no need to do that. Why spoil it for your parents now? They'll be back from their honeymoon soon. Hopefully Alex should be more like his old self, so why knock him for six when there's no need? All I ask is you start behaving more affectionately towards me in public until the New Year. No big deal.'

'I'll try,' she said quietly, realising defeat once more. Perhaps what he was suggesting wasn't as outrageous as she had first thought. Maybe society women did that sort of thing all the time, for fun — a prank, and thought nothing of it.

'You know you're truly beautiful, Lexie,' he said softly as if it was a secret between them, 'especially when you smile. That was what I noticed when we first met — the warmth and sincerity of your smile. And even when the going was tough, you managed to remain outwardly unruffled and calm, although I can imagine what you were feeling underneath. I admire the way you faced up to everything. It can't have been easy coping with Bay View's problems, especially at your age.

'Now, to a more mundane subject. I've arranged for a new assistant to start next week to take over from Polly so you can have a more roving role in the running of the hotel. Sandra is fully competent to do reception work, and has excellent references, so I believe she'll fit in very nicely. Will that suit you better?'

'Yes, I suppose so.' She smiled

half-heartedly, biting her lip in an attempt to hold back the tears. His compliments were so unexpected. He didn't think she was completely useless.

'I thought it would be more in keeping with what you did at Bay View. It will also take some of the pressure off me and give me more time to get on with another project I have in mind. I didn't realise how you felt about your role at Thornton Grange. I was letting you settle in and find your feet with what's obviously quite a different setup from what you're used to. You've coped extremely well. Come the New Year, we'll have to have a major review about the running of Thornton Grange, but until then I hope we can manage.'

'I guess I'm not used to taking orders,' she said, recovering somewhat. Maybe she could manage a bite to eat after all. The melon looked delicious.

'At Thornton Grange, as you must have realised by now, we don't have any set duties as such,' he said, obviously trying to find a safe topic of conversation. 'By that I mean all the staff can and should take over from anybody else at a moment's notice. No demarcation. I know it doesn't cover every eventuality, but I believe all my staff should make a contribution if they see the need for an extra pair of hands. It's not unknown for me to act as barman, I'll have you know, although I've not been called on to act as chambermaid yet!'

She could well imagine him behind the bar serving drinks. He probably was very good at anything he put his mind to, as Alex told her. They began discussing the change in her duties and problems to do with the forthcoming Christmas house-party and New Year package. Once they got on to the more ordinary work topics, Lexie managed to relax a little. Jake could be quite charming when he wanted to be, and she wondered if that was because of Alex's influence.

By the time they left the restaurant, she was feeling more at ease about the whole situation and accepted his arm around her waist as part of the performance she had elected to participate in. The wine certainly helped, and it was comforting having a man treat her with such propriety. Now she realised why she hadn't enjoyed the advances made by previous boyfriends. They had been crude and immature by comparison. Jake had the knack of treating her like a lady.

Back at the hotel, he was in time to help her from the car since she had a struggle with the seat belt. Instead of stepping away from him though, she found herself entangled in his arms. She looked up in consternation, feeling gauche and clumsy, just when she'd been wanting to create a good impression. Then the stars were blotted out as he claimed a kiss — their first kiss. His lips covering hers were soft, teasing and unbelievably satisfying. Taken by surprise, momentarily off guard, she found herself responding, finding it indeed pleasurable as she had once hypothesised. The kiss deepened as he nibbled her lip and his tongue demanded entry, setting up a whole new wave of emotions. She clung to him, moaning softly as he teased and demanded, cajoled and conquered. It was all so new and agreeably satisfying.

His arms crushed her against his chest, making her whimper. Somehow her hands found their way unwittingly round his neck and her body melted against his, aflame with desire. She was literally quivering with a deep, over-whelming longing. It occurred to her hazily that it must be love to make her so sensitive. No man had ever made her feel so alive before; so aware of every tingling nerve throughout her whole body. Just one kiss — that was all it took. Talk about the earth moving. Her legs felt too weak to support her.

How long she remained there hanging on to him, oblivious to their surroundings, she didn't know. It could have been minutes or hours. His next remark brought her to earth with a bump.

'Now you look like a fiancée.'

Letting go of her, he led her into the hotel. If he had slapped her face, she couldn't have felt more ashamed. The kiss meant nothing to him! It was only part of the charade. How could he! How could he! Once inside she couldn't escape, as he kept tight hold of her hand and laughingly led her into the office.

'You haven't got into your role properly yet, have you? Didn't you see the way Polly was watching?'

'I'm sorry.' Her cheeks burned with embarrassment and indignation. What would he think of her clinging to him like that? She didn't know what had come over her. Never in her whole life had she been so humiliated.

'I'll escort you upstairs, and tomorrow you can act the excited fiancée.' He kissed her again, only this time a light teasing kiss hardly brushing her lips; and with hands entwined they went upstairs together. Fortunately Polly was occupied with a guest at the time and smiled a greeting as they passed.

'Relax. I'll only stay a moment. Just long enough to set the scene.' He walked over to the window and stared moodily out across the car park, unconsciously jangling keys in his pocket.

Why couldn't she get it through her thick skull it was all a farce? Lexie numbly removed her jacket and slumped onto the chair, feeling thoroughly drained. What on earth had possessed her to do such a thing? If that was what love did to you, then she didn't want anything to do with it. It was all totally alien, and she felt out of control.

When he had gone, she undressed and had a shower to try to calm her agonised feelings, letting the water drown out her thoughts for a long, long time before crawling into bed. Her emotions were all mixed up as she remembered the wonderful passionate response Jake's kisses stirred up. How could she find them enjoyable? It was so inconceivable — so disastrous. She must never let it happen again.

It took her ages to get to sleep. She kept going over and over in her mind what Jake expected her to do. How could she appear loving towards him when in private he was so hard and uncompromising? Why did he want her to act such a part? He still hadn't told her. Round and round her thoughts spiralled. Finally she dropped into a restless sleep, tossing and turning for the remainder of the night. She dreamt about being back at Bay View, and the bank manager was there at the front door barring her way. He told her she couldn't go in as the bank now owned the property. Then Jake appeared in the form of the devil. He said of course she could come in, but there would have to be conditions. 'You belong to me, Lexie Prescott,' he said. 'You will have to do everything I tell you — no questions asked.' She awoke, hot and yet shivery.

It was a very nervous Lexie who went down to breakfast wearing her engagement ring for all the staff to see. She accepted their congratulations, smiling ruefully at some of the wisecracks made about her marrying the boss. Fortunately it was Polly's day off, so she had time to get used to her new role before having to explain things to her. Since her arrival at Thornton Grange, she had got on well with Polly. She enjoyed their chats, so particularly disliked the idea of deceiving her. It hadn't proved as difficult as she had expected in the staffroom, so she went to take her place at the reception desk feeling somewhat relieved.

'Good morning, darling.' Jake approached her unnoticed.

'Good morning, Jake. How are you this morning?' she managed to say in a calm, normal voice.

'All the better for seeing you with a smile on your face,' he replied. 'I take it you've set the gossip alive in the staffroom?'

'Yes. That's what you wanted, isn't it?'

He fingered her hand with the ring on it and looked quizzically at her. 'We shall need your room for Sandra when she arrives. In the circumstances, I think it best if you move into the spare bedroom in my annexe flat.'

'Surely there must be other rooms available,' she stammered, wide-eyed with consternation. Why did he keep unsettling her, seemingly on purpose, and enjoying her discomfiture? 'I'll check, shall I?'

'Don't bother. I want you to occupy my spare room until after Christmas. Here's the key. You can move in whenever you like. Sandra will be here next week — Wednesday probably. The other key is for the door to the fire escape, by the way.'

He moved away as a guest approached, and Lexie concentrated on her work, helping with a bus timetable and the times of the steamers on Lake Windermere. When she had a moment, she looked over the lists for the Christmas period and saw the hotel was indeed full — not a spare bed anywhere. She sighed resignedly. She would have to put up with bossy Jake for a little while longer, but one day she would tell him exactly what she thought of him!

# 7

Jake too was having all sorts of conflicting emotions. He didn't know why he had behaved as he had. At first he was simply annoyed at Lexie's association with Jackson, but the more he thought about it the more he realised it wasn't the complete truth. He'd been dying to kiss her ever since their first meeting, but he hadn't been prepared for her response. He had expected a cold rebuff at least, if not a slap on the face for his effrontery. He certainly had not expected her to respond so passionately.

She had looked stunned too, as if she couldn't believe the powerful feelings erupting between them. It hadn't been the response of a naive young innocent either. Just what sort of game was she playing? he wondered. They'd see how she coped with the more demanding duties he'd imposed, he thought. That should show him what she was made of. He smiled to himself when he thought about what she was going to have to contend with in the next few weeks, and wondered if he shouldn't have warned her. It probably wasn't a good idea having her in his private apartment, but he couldn't alter that now. It was only until after the New Year, and they would both be busy.

*   *   *

Lexie went to investigate the flat as soon as she was relieved. Having seen Jake go out, she knew it was an opportune moment to have a look round on her own. She had been curious about the flat ever since Debbie mentioned how marvellous it was, but she hadn't had an occasion to see it for herself until now. Unlocking the communicating door, she had the strange feeling of being an intruder. She had Jake's permission, but it was

163

like stepping into his private world — invading his privacy. She almost retreated, thinking it would be better to wait until he was around, but a movement caught her eye. It was a cat. A large ginger cat which stared at her before stalking haughtily into a room at the end of the narrow hallway.

Quickly she closed the door and went to see where he had gone. It turned out to be the lounge — and what a lounge! She gazed in wonder at its lavish furnishings, surprised to see a real log fire burning in the grate. The leather sofa looked sumptuously soft and luxurious, and yet the sheepskin rug in front of the fire gave the room a welcoming, homely feel. The cat was washing itself on the hearth rug and paused long enough to observe her presence before carrying on with its ablutions unperturbed.

A sliding patio door gave access to a small veranda and a fire escape from which the view was tremendous. In such an elevated position, it was a panorama of fells with the lake a perfect jewel in the valley bottom. How lucky he was to have such a wonderful place to live, she thought enviously; and the flat in Ravenstone too.

She went in search of her bedroom, wondering what delights it contained if the rest of the flat was anything to go by. The first door opened on to Jake's bedroom, by the look of the masculine attire adorning the valet, so she hastily closed it and tried the next. This looked like the spare room. It had a double bed with a wine-coloured padded head-board and chintz duvet matching the curtains. Her feet sank into the soft cream carpet. On either side of the bed were small bedside tables on which resided antique brass lamps with deep pink shades. A wardrobe fitted into one alcove, and across the corner of the room was a heart-shaped dressing table complete with frilly drapes. It was a charmingly feminine room, absolutely enchanting. Everything looked new and unused, as if waiting for someone special for which it had been designed. She wondered who that person was and why it hadn't been occupied. Had it been for someone he loved? She was still left wondering who he was deceiving. She knew so little about Jake apart from what Alex had told her initially. Perhaps she ought to ask Polly sometime — discreetly of course.

'Will it do?' The softly spoken words alarmed her.

She spun round to find Jake watching her as she trailed fingers along the window ledge, lost in thought. 'Oh, yes.' She realised she had spent far too long there. 'I'm sorry, I was daydreaming. It's fine. Quite lovely.'

'Fancy a cup of coffee? I was going to make one.'

'Err . . . yes please,' she stammered, and followed him into the small kitchenette where he produced the necessary equipment with practised ease.

'What do you think of my home from home?'

'To tell the truth, it's absolutely fantastic,' she admitted, feeling slightly more comfortable in the domesticity of the kitchen. 'You'd never know what was going on on the other side of that door, would you? A sanctuary of tranquillity. You're very fortunate.' She knew it made her sound jealous, but it was the truth.

'You had it pretty tough at Bay View, didn't you?'

'It was hard being on duty almost twenty-four hours a day seven days a week. We couldn't afford to employ many staff latterly, so we had to cover it full-time ourselves, and of course the only privacy we had was our small sitting room, which wasn't exactly isolated from the rest of the hotel as you well know.'

'Why didn't you pull out sooner when all the other hotels changed over?' he asked, raising his voice above the noise of the percolator.

'You know how it is. It has been in the Prescott family for so long we were reluctant to sell, and yet we couldn't afford the necessary alterations to make it viable. It was the usual catch twenty-two problem. I suppose we should have made the break when my grandparents died, but . . . well, we didn't.'

He carried the coffee into the lounge, motioning her to find a seat. 'I hope you'll make full use of the flat to relax more in your off-duty hours. We shouldn't get in each other's way, and maybe it will help with your play-acting. This, by the way,' he added, picking up the cat and settled it on his knee, 'is Sebastian. He adopted me. Just wandered in one day and took up residence.'

'He's gorgeous. Is he friendly?'

'He doesn't take to everyone, but I find he's good company. He doesn't cost much to keep and he doesn't ask much of me. Do you, Sebastian, old boy?' He tickled the cat's head and it purred noisily, settling down with obvious contentment. It knew when he was on to a good thing. Lexie smothered a chuckle, though, when Sebastian showed his approval by digging his claws in. Jake promptly disengaged the cat and placed him on the floor with the threat of having his claws trimmed before he was much older.

Lexie took a sip of coffee. Since Jake's arrival, the flat had taken on a completely different character. It was almost electrifying. She felt a sort of animal magnetism that alarmed her. The episode the previous night hadn't affected him, apparently; not in the way it affected her, at any rate. He was behaving quite normally, as if she was simply a member of staff. She was dimly aware of Jake continuing saying she was welcome to make herself the odd snack if she felt like it instead of using the staffroom.

'I have a maid come in every morning to tidy round and restock the fridge. Lexie, are you listening? You look as if you were off in a daydream again.'

'Yes, I'm listening,' she replied, blinking rapidly. 'I'm sorry, I was wondering what Bay View was like now and whether the ground floor flat was going to be ready in time. They'll be home soon.'

'We'll go over at the first opportunity,' he promised. 'The architect tells me all is going well and it will be ready according to plan — wonders never cease! But to put your mind at rest, we will have a run over to see for ourselves.'

'I could go on my own on my next day off,' she said quickly, thinking she should have thought of that before. She could always hire a car.

'It would be better if we both go, and I could do with a talk to the architect anyway,' he added, leaving her no room for dissension.

Lexie finished her coffee and got to her feet. 'I'd better be going.'

'Don't go on my account. Why not pack your things and move in straight away. It will give them longer to get your room ready for Sandra. You'll make sure you keep the doors locked at all times, won't you? I value my privacy here and don't want to find unexpected guests wandering round. This is my home, not just an extension to the hotel.'

He made everything sound so reasonable! Why did she feel he was manipulating her all the time? He got up and collected the coffee cups to take back to the kitchen, and she made her escape, calling out she would see him later. Back in her own bedroom, she stood looking out of the window with unseeing eyes. Her thoughts were all on how she was going to keep her serenity when every time she came into contact with Jake he had such a bizarre effect on her. She wished she could understand her own feelings. She had never felt like this about anyone before. What was it about him that attracted her when he was such a bossy individual?

She packed her case and resolutely went back to Jake's flat. She would have to act her part for another month, and then she would be able to go back to living her own life again. She wondered how they would be able to work together when they became unengaged, but since Jake had got them into this situation then he could jolly well find a way out of it. She smiled to herself, thinking perhaps she wouldn't have to stay working for him much longer, and certainly not until the completion of the all the flats, because he surely wouldn't relish her still being at Thornton Grange when they broke off their engagement.

The next morning she was up early, spending the minimum of time in the bathroom before dressing and scurrying downstairs for breakfast. It was only when she bumped into Polly outside the staffroom that she remembered she still had to face her barrage of questions.

'Hi there. What's this I hear? Gossip has it you've managed to ensnare the boss. So that was why you were all dressed up the other evening. I should have known. Let's have a look at the ring.' Polly was ecstatic. 'Wow! However did you manage it? Wait until Miss Trufitt hears about this. You sly fox! You never gave us an inkling this was on the cards. How long has this been going on? I thought you had just met and had you pegged as Simon Jackson's girl.'

Lexie smiled ruefully. 'Simon's a good friend, that's all. But who's Miss Trufitt when she's at home?'

They helped themselves to breakfast off the side table and found a place setting by the window. As soon as they sat down, Polly informed her she had better watch out. 'Miss Camilla Trufitt was your predecessor. She's the only daughter of the Trufitts, who live at the big old house on the far side of the lake. You know, the one with the imposing gates and the extensive shrubbery. They also have a flat in London and a villa in Spain, I believe. They drop in here quite often for drinks or a meal when they're home. They're good friends of Jake's — at least Joe and his wife are; I don't know about Camilla. We'll have to wait and see how the land lies there.'

'How do you mean my predecessor?' Lexie asked, trying to sound unconcerned, but she could feel her stomach turn tipple-tails. Was she installed in Camilla's room? 'Was Jake engaged to Miss Trufitt or something?'

'Oh yes, indeed he was! Miss High and Mighty came in here flaunting a ring the size of a golf ball and straight away flounced around giving orders as if she was taking over. She was an absolute b . . .' Polly was in full sway in her inimitable way. Lexie knew she should have stopped her. She felt disloyal for listening to gossip, but wanted to know all the same, and Jake was hardly likely to tell her.

'What happened?' she asked, carefully spreading marmalade on her toast with great precision.

'Well, most of it is only rumour. Apparently Camilla first made a play for the doctor. I say that's rather good, because it's where they met — acting in the village play. Anyway, next she set her sights on Jake because he was obviously wealthier — she's that sort of woman. Gossip has it he only went out with her because of her father, but she seemed to twist him round her little finger — heaven knows how.'

Lexie's eyes widened. Anyone who could twist Jake round their little finger was going to be quite a woman!

'They hadn't been going out long,' Polly said somewhat grimly, 'when she comes in flashing an engagement ring. She immediately started lording it over us lower minions like a harridan. She really was obnoxious.'

'What happened?' Lexie asked. She had stopped all pretence of disinterest.

'One day she left. Just upped and went.' Polly sniffed in disgust and speared the egg on her plate venomously. 'Along with an American millionaire who happened to be staying here. Nobody actually saw them leave, but one only had to put two and two together to know what happened. It was too much of a coincidence.'

'What did Jake do? It must have been terrible for him.' Lexie could imagine the devastating effect it would have on Jake to be so humiliated.

'Jake wasn't here at the time, but that wouldn't bother Camilla. She doesn't care about hurting anyone's feelings. She would trample all over anyone without a single thought. All she wants is money and prestige — love doesn't come into it. When Jake returned, you can imagine how he felt. Everyone knew what had happened, it was so obvious, but he didn't show it — not one iota. He continued as if nothing had changed, but it made its mark, I do assure you. No man enjoys being made a fool of, and Jake is a proud man.'

Lexie nodded her head thoughtfully. 'When did all this happen?'

'Earlier this year. Round about the time he lost his mother, I think it was. That was why he wasn't here. It's been a bad time for him, one way or another.

Anyway, what I'm getting round to in my own roundabout way is the latest news, which is that she — Camilla — is home for Christmas. Apparently the creep she went off with has ditched her, so perhaps she's returned to restore her pride by going after Jake again. Everyone here was beginning to feel a shade apprehensive, wondering how Jake would take it and whether he would have her back. I for one didn't think he would. To tell the truth, I think some of the staff were ready to hand in their notices, it really was that bad. Now we haven't anything to worry about, have we? I'm absolutely thrilled to bits you two are going to make a go of it. You have a lot in common after all, and you look right together. I'm only sorry I won't be around for the wedding. I trust you'll send me an invitation though. Maybe I can wangle a trip home, you never know. Gosh, is that the time?'

There was a mad scramble to go on duty, so the conversation had to lapse at

177

that point, but Lexie understood what Jake really wanted her to do — she was protecting him from the clutches of his ex-fiancée! No wonder the staff looked so relieved at the news of their engagement, if what Polly said was true.

For the rest of the morning, Lexie concentrated on her work; and rather than have lunch in the staffroom, she went back to the flat to prepare a snack while she digested what Polly had told her. She didn't like listening to rumours and wondered how much of what Polly had said was true. Was Jake still carrying a torch for Camilla but not wanting to be hurt again? She wouldn't have thought he would need to stoop to such trickery, and felt there must be some other reason for his behaviour. She hadn't anticipated Jake being there in the flat.

'Care to join me? I was only going to rustle up some scrambled eggs. I can soon make enough for two.'

It seemed churlish to refuse. 'Lovely. I didn't know you could cook.'

'There's a lot you don't know about me,' he replied quietly. His mood was amiable, so she felt it was an opportunity to let him know she sympathised with his situation.

'I've been learning though,' she said, and watched his expression.

He didn't appear dismayed. In fact he looked remarkably calm. Only by the slightest shrug of his shoulders did he show he was in any way annoyed. 'Oh. So now what's the grapevine been telling you?' he asked, deftly whisking the eggs and popping bread in the toaster. 'It's amazing how news spreads around here and gets distorted,' he emphasised.

'I know why you want a fiancée all of a sudden.' She decided to take the bull by the horns and have it all out in the open so she knew where she stood. She would be better able to help him if she knew the truth.

'Would you care to set the table? Then maybe we can continue this intriguing conversation over lunch. I might have known Polly would put you in the picture, but she does like to embroider everything.'

Lexie set the small table in the corner of the lounge with the cutlery and crockery he handed her and made the tea while he dished up the eggs.

'Voila! I can cook eggs if nothing else,' he declared, placing a plate piled high with the buttery scrambled eggs on the table.

Lexie complimented him generously, particularly on the dash of cinnamon he'd added and the touch of parsley.

'Now then, what have you been learning about me this morning that's put a frown on your face?'

He was in such a good mood she didn't want to upset him, so she didn't know how to phrase her reply. 'Polly told me about Camilla Trufitt — your ex-fiancée.' Lexie's lips curled contemptuously; even the name sounded conceited and snobbish.

'I see. So now you want my version, is that it?' He frowned into his teacup as if deciding how much to tell her. 'OK. So you've heard about Camilla. For my part, that's finished — all over and forgotten. It was about the time I felt unsettled by the death of my mother and the problems Alex was having. I wasn't thinking straight. Camilla and I went about for a while, but then someone more interesting came along so she left. I guess you could say a woman's wiles bewitched me when I was at my most vulnerable. It was something I vowed would never happen again. However,' he said, turning to face her, 'I've since heard she's back, staying with her parents for the holidays, and I'd rather not have any unpleasantness. Not,' he added with a wry smile, 'because of our previous relationship, but because her father and I may do business together. I don't want to spoil my association with him by declining to co-operate with his mercurial, fickle daughter. Does that answer your questions?'

'I wish you'd told me this before,

instead of having to learn it of it by rumour and supposition,' Lexie murmured. It gave a slightly differenct slant to things.

'Would you have gone along with it any differently? I need to get through the Christmas period with some sort of relief,' he said wearily. 'I've got a lot on my mind at present and was trying to take the easy way out — trying to put a stop to Camilla's antics before they begin. Once you meet her you'll understand.'

'I understand now the why, but have you thought about what happens later when we split up? I shan't be able to stay on here then, shall I?'

'Don't worry about that for the moment. I want to get over the next few weeks in as calm a state as I can. Rather a lot is riding on this deal, and I don't want Camilla fouling things up.'

Lexie smiled at him, for the first time realising he felt vulnerable, particularly when dealing with women, and needed her help. The great Jake Thornton actually needed her help!

'I'll carry out my part of the bargain. I promised I would, and I don't go back on promises no matter how difficult they become,' she said, collecting the dirty plates together. The atmosphere in the flat suddenly didn't seem so oppressive. In fact it was quite pleasant washing up in the closeness of the kitchenette. Afterwards, before returning to duty, they sat in the lounge discussing the return of the honeymooners and the Christmas festivities. In his more amenable moods, she found Jake very agreeable company — too agreeable for her own comfort, maybe!

★   ★   ★

Two days later, Lexie met Miss Camilla Trufitt. She was alone at reception standing in while Polly had a break. A petite redhead stalked in imperiously, demanding to see the hotel manager. Lexie summed her up as a troublemaker before she even opened her mouth, so wasn't surprised to discover who she was.

'Can I help you? I'm afraid Mr Thornton isn't available at the moment. He's in a meeting.'

The woman glared at Lexie with undisguised dislike, apparently appalled by the suggestion she could in any way stand in for Jake. 'I wish to speak to Jake personally. Please inform him I will await him in the cocktail bar.'

'Whom shall I say is asking for him?' Lexie continued to hold her composure, although bristling with annoyance.

'You're obviously new here, but it may interest you to know I'm his fiancée, so don't be impertinent or you may find yourself out of a job.' And with that stinging retort, Miss Trufitt turned and sauntered into the bar.

So that was the ex-fiancée! Wow. Lexie was looking forward to wiping the smug look off the woman's face. How could Jake ever have got entangled with such a woman? He normally had such

excellent choice, but there again Camilla was definitely eye-catching, and she
certainly had a good figure; one had to
admit that. If one liked the pouting type
of female viper, Camilla was an
excellent choice. Calmly picking up the
telephone, Lexie called Jake, who was
in conference in the flat. He'd given
instructions not to be disturbed, but
she didn't know if that applied to
Camilla. Besides, she felt he ought to be
informed of her presence in the hotel in
case he wanted to avoid her.

'Jake, your ex-fiancée is expecting
you to join her in the cocktail bar,
pronto.' She stressed the 'ex' part but
didn't wait for the expletive which no
doubt followed. Shortly afterwards,
though, she was flabbergasted to see
Jake striding across the foyer to the bar.
So much for not wanting to be
disturbed! So Camilla was important
after all, was she? She would love to be
a fly on the wall to witness their
renewed acquaintance with each other,
especially when he advised her of the

185

recent alteration to his matrimonial position. Would she make a scene?

Debbie arrived. 'Mr Thornton's compliments, and would you join him in the bar?'

Lexie wanted to refuse but knew she couldn't. She didn't like disputes, but maybe in this case she could make an exception. This, after all, was why she was wearing Jake's ring. Maybe once Miss Trufitt learnt Jake was no longer the eligible bachelor, she would take off and the charade will be over. Lexie wasn't sure if she wanted to part with the ring so soon. She had grown attached to it. She certainly didn't wish to have anything to do with Miss Trufitt. Having met her, she knew she wasn't going to like her. It had been an instinctive dislike which she didn't think would improve with time, and she only hoped their meetings in future would be few and far between. Taking a deep breath, she straightened her jacket and walked confidently into the bar with as broad a smile as she could manage.

'There you are, darling.' Jake rose to greet her, kissing her lightly on the cheek. 'I want you to meet an old friend, Camilla Trufitt. Camilla, this is my fiancée, Lexie.'

If looks could kill, Lexie would have been struck dead on the spot. The announcement was clearly news to Camilla — devastating news.

'Lexie has taken over all the arrangements and bookings for Christmas,' Jake was saying, apparently oblivious to Camilla's wrath, while Lexie watched the colour drain from her face and felt a twinge of vindictive pleasure. 'Camilla was hoping to book in for the holiday, but I've told her we're full up. That is still the position, isn't it?'

'Yes, of course it is, Jake. We could have filled the hotel twice over with the number we've turned away.' Lexie was determined to play her role to perfection in front of this cold, calculating woman. Polly told her she had nearly caused a mass walk-out by the staff and it was easy to see why.

'There, you see? You should have contacted us earlier. You'll just have to come for a few meals. Chef is excelling himself with his highly acclaimed menus. I'm sure we can squeeze another table in somehow. I presume you're staying with your parents?'

Lexie was amazed how quickly Camilla recovered from such an appalling discovery. It must have been a severe blow to her pride following so soon from her last admirer's rejection. Ignoring Lexie, she spoke directly to Jake. 'Huh. I don't know how they talked me into spending Christmas at home this year. They've got a lot of doddering old relatives visiting so I thought I'd escape here. I'd much rather be skiing in Switzerland or basking on some Hawaiian beach. This isn't my scene at all, and if you won't find me a room, I might take off again.'

'I'm sure your parents must be delighted you came home,' Jake replied, continuing to stand next to Lexie; he gave her hand a friendly squeeze. 'Your mother will be especially pleased to have you help entertain the guests, since the last time I saw her she wasn't feeling well. I'm afraid, as I told you though, we haven't a spare room anywhere in the hotel until after the festivities.'

'Jake, if there's nothing else, I ought to go and relieve Debbie. We're rather busy at the moment and a little short-handed.' Lexie couldn't wait to get away. As far as Camilla was concerned, she was redundant anyway.

'Yes of course, love. I'll see you at lunch.'

Lexie smiled sweetly at Camilla. 'Nice to have met you, Miss Trufitt. I'm sorry we can't be of more assistance.' As she left, she heard Camilla's whining voice saying that she thought Jake would have made an exception in her case. She even had the temerity to ask about the spare room in his flat. Lexie smiled inwardly, realising how astute Jake had been. If she knew all about the spare room, then perhaps she had organised the furnishing of it. It had a definite woman's touch.

At lunch time, Lexie joined Jake in the flat, where he was still entertaining the business acquaintance. The meeting had been delayed by the arrival of Camilla, so they had a meal sent up from the kitchen for the three of them. Lexie hadn't had time to ask if he wanted to be alone with his guest, so she tried not to be intrusive, but Jake made a great display of including her in the conversation, much to her surprise. George Grant looked like a middle-aged businessman, probably happily married with a couple of teenage children, Lexie thought; and it transpired she was fairly accurate with her conjecture. He also came from near Ravenstone, so they spent some time happily reminiscing about people and places they both knew.

As soon as lunch was cleared away, Lexie made her escape, leaving the men to their discussion over coffee. She went down to the staffroom, where she found Polly with her feet up.

'What did you think of her?' she asked with a mischievous grin as soon as Lexie walked in the door.

'Now I wonder who you could be meaning?' Lexie remarked dryly. 'You wouldn't by any chance be referring to the Lady Camilla, would you?'

'Got it in one. I knew it wouldn't be long before she came skulking round here hoping to pick up where she left off. She thinks she only has to snap her fingers to have men running to her side. I hope Jake has more sense now and can see through her little game.'

Lexie flopped down in a chair and ran a hand through her hair. 'All I can say is Jake had one very lucky escape. How he ever got entangled with the likes of her I'll never know. He's not usually so blind. How could such a pint-sized shrew get her own way with him?'

'You wait and see!' warned Polly. 'You haven't seen the last of her, so watch out. I would hate to see you come unstuck, and she will have the knives out for you, my girl. She has influence around here, being Joe Trufitt's daughter — his only daughter, and his pride and joy.'

Lexie shivered theatrically. 'Enough about her. Jake told her what's what and put her in her place. I only hope we don't see too much of her while she's home, although she intends making use of the facilities, I gather. Now, when did you say you were leaving? I'm going to miss you.'

# 8

'We'll go over to Ravenstone on Friday,' Jake announced. 'Make sure we're covered, will you? It will probably be the last chance we get to have any time off before Christmas.'

'I'll see what I can do, but now that Polly has left, we'll be a bit stretched until Sandra takes over,' Lexie replied.

'Sandra's due in today, isn't she?' he queried. 'See if she'll start early. You're obviously dying to see Bay View again, and your folks will be back next week. I'd like to see all's well, although they intend staying here until after New Year, I believe.'

When Sandra Morris arrived, Lexie was by happy coincidence in the reception area, so she personally escorted her up to her old room. 'I hope you'll like working here. You're starting at a busy time.'

'I'm sure I'll be fine. I feel very lucky having such a marvellous opportunity. I've always loved this part of the country, ever since I came here as a child. Not that we could afford to stay anywhere as grand as Thornton Grange,' she said obsequiously. 'To me this is a dream come true, to be able to live and work in such superb surroundings. I remember it before its renovations, of course. Mr Thornton has done a grand job and no mistake.'

Lexie concurred. 'Could you possibly start tomorrow instead of Monday, do you think?'

'Why sure, that's no problem. I'd probably be mooching about the village, so I may as well be working,' Sandra agreed amicably. 'I'll have plenty of time to look up old friends now I'm here.'

'Well that's a relief. Mr Thornton and I want to go off for the day on Friday, so it gives us tomorrow to show you the ropes. I gather you're fully conversant with this type of work?'

'Oh yes. I've worked at the Green Man in Dunstan, and the Clifton in Summerbridge. It shouldn't take me long to get to grips with your system. I'm not local, but I've been coming to this part of the Lake District for such a long time I feel I should be able to answer the guests' queries.'

Lexie left her to settle in. She seemed an admirable choice, pleasant in a homely way, yet with a quiet confidence about her. Her clothes were serviceable and neat and her general manner welcoming and friendly. Lexie felt sure she would fit in with the rest of the staff and acknowledged once again Jake knew his business.

★　★　★

On Friday it was still dark when they set off, because Jake wanted to be in Ravenstone by late morning. It would be a long trip there and back in the day. The roads were reasonably clear of traffic, but there was a hint of frost, and

Lexie was conscious of Jake having to concentrate on his driving, so she settled back to listen to the cassette he was playing. She liked his choice of music — that was one thing they did have in common. She had been getting worked up at the prospect of spending a whole day with Jake — alone, especially the journey time. Three or more hours cooped up with him was enough to make anyone apprehensive. It proved to be an uneventful trip however, and they pulled up outside Bay View on the stroke of eleven o' clock.

'Not bad timing,' he observed. 'Coffee time.'

Lexie extricated herself from the car and stretched. She breathed in deeply the fresh sea air, then hurriedly pulled her coat close round her. It felt decidedly chilly. It seemed strange to be back in Ravenstone. In the few short weeks she'd spent at Thornton Grange, Lexie had come to appreciate and love it. Now Ravenstone, and more to the point Bay View, lacked a certain something even though it was her home.

Bay View didn't look much different from the outside, but the change was soon apparent when they entered the front door. Her parents' flat was almost ready for occupation. The decorators were putting the finishing touches to the hallway, but all the other rooms were now decorated and carpeted, awaiting the arrival of furniture, some of which was temporarily housed in an upstairs room. Lexie was amazed at how much had been achieved in three months. Her part of the flat had been completed too. She thought it looked wonderful, and was rather pleased with her choice, and wished Jake would show some sign of approval. He walked throughout with an air of almost impatience, but critical all the same. She had a job keeping up with him.

'I was going to use some of the carpeting from the lounge to go down in my room,' Lexie said with a frown. 'I see now they've used the same as for the rest of the flat. I should have been here to see to it.'

'It looks fine to me,' Jake said, glancing at the new bathroom.

'I know, but I wasn't going to impose on your generosity for anything for my room,' Lexie muttered.

'Most unusual,' was his dry comment as he headed for the upstairs flat.

Lexie followed, a bit miffed.

'I think it would be best if Alex and Jessica choose the furniture themselves after all, don't you?' Jake said. 'They could always stay at the Royal until it's ready for occupation.'

'You're probably right,' she sighed. OK, so it wasn't exactly lavish like his establishment, she thought grimly, but she had kept a tight rein on finances. She felt she had achieved a splendid result relatively inexpensively and knew it would be what her mother would approve of.

'Let's go and see if they've done any work to the top flat,' Jake urged her on, obviously not wishing to spend too long in Ravenstone; he had told her it was to be a flying visit. That suited her. She had thought she would be pleased to see her old home and eager to return, but that wasn't how it struck her at all. It seemed strange going out of the flat to gain access to the lift area and the main staircase. When they arrived at the top of the house, they found not a lot had changed. They would have to make alterations to the roof, and that would be best done when the winter was over, she realised.

'I like what I've seen of the plans for up here,' she said, wandering into the room which had been hers since childhood.

'The architect certainly seems to have some bright ideas, I'll grant you, but so he should for what he's charging,' Jake remarked. 'Still, he was a good choice thanks to you. Have you any suggestions for the decor for here? You obviously have an eye for colour.'

'I . . . I don't know . . . I presumed you would . . . '

'Just wondered,' he murmured, inspecting a stain on the ceiling. 'It's not too important for the moment.'

Lexie looked out on the well-remembered view. The sweep of the sandy bay to the rocky headland and the lighthouse standing proudly at its farthest extremity. Even at this time of year it was a fascinating scene — a scene she never grew tired of whatever the weather. This was what she was going to miss most. It had greeted her every morning for as long as she could remember. She felt she knew every inch of the bay. She recalled the time she sat with her grandfather watching the Northern Lights. What a spectacle that had been, something she would never forget. And the time a storm beached a tanker in the bay — fortunately it had been re-floated without too much damage, but it had been headline news. From her vantage point, she could pinpoint most of Ravenstone's principal buildings and see the cliff paths she had rambled along in her carefree days as a child. So many memories, some happy, some sad.

'I suppose these were staff quarters in the old days,' Jake mused, drifting over to the window to stand beside her. 'They had a splendid view if nothing else.'

'Yes,' she said sadly, and walked away to start opening drawers and stacking clothes ready to take back with her. Nothing stayed the same. One had to learn to accept what life had to offer in the way of change. This past year had seen many unexpected changes, and she couldn't say they were all unwelcome. What the future held for her was in the lap of the gods — or at least Jake for the moment.

After speaking to the builders who were busy in various parts of the other flats, they called on the architect and then went for a late lunch.

'Sorry you won't have time to look up any of your friends this trip, Lexie,' Jake said as they left the restaurant.

'That doesn't matter,' she replied.

'There's no one I particularly wish to see.'

To which he raised an eyebrow but said nothing. She guessed he was thinking about Nigel, and she definitely didn't want to meet him again just yet. The weather had turned dismal and wet, so they weren't inclined to linger over lunch, and soon were heading west. This time, however, Jake took a different route out of Ravenstone. Lexie was about to mention he'd taken a wrong turning, but then thought better of it, which was just as well.

Shortly afterwards, he said, 'There's something I want to look at while I'm over here. It won't take us much out of our way, so it won't make us too late back. You don't mind, do you?'

'Not at all,' she replied, knowing full well it wouldn't make a scrap of difference if she had. She felt depressed. Whether it was the poor weather or because her feelings for Jake were so mixed up, she didn't know; but after seeing her old bedroom, she felt miserable. Since Jake had arrived on the scene, her whole life had been turned upside-down, although to be honest she knew it was really Alex who had brought about the change. The arrival of her father had set in motion a string of circumstances, which if she could have foreseen . . . would she have done any different? She doubted it. In some ways life was now much more exciting — at least, it was definitely more unpredictable.

They travelled about twenty miles or so before Jake pulled onto a minor country road, and shortly afterwards stopped the car in the entrance to a field. She couldn't think what there was to interest him in such a deserted place — just fields, woods and an old dilapidated farmhouse. Perhaps he was revisiting some place — some child-hood memory, trying to recapture something from his past, she thought. Alex had said he was born on a farm, didn't he? Maybe this was it.

'Shan't be long,' he said, grabbing his

coat from behind the seats. Shrugging into it, he strode purposefully out of sight. He didn't ask her to accompany him, and she didn't feel inclined to get out into the cold to see what else there was. Maybe he would deign to enlighten her when he returned — if he found what he was looking for, she thought.

It was nearly ten minutes later before Jake returned, letting in an icy draught as he threw his coat in first.

'Have you plans to become a farmer now?' she quizzed, since he remained silently surveying the scene through the rain-speckled windscreen.

'No,' came the brusque reply; and without further ado, he set the car in motion and reversed out into the lane. He looked preoccupied, and remained so for a long time; and since he obviously didn't wish to communicate further, Lexie sat in huffy silence, staring unseeingly at the scenery. The only sound was the swish of the windscreen wipers and the tyres on the wet road. Some little while later, Jake suggested she find some music to play; a more conciliatory mood had returned. She selecting a Beethoven symphony.

'What sort of music do you like, Lexie? Any particular favourites?'

'Mostly classical,' she murmured. 'I'm not much into the modern stuff, I'm afraid. I don't mind a little country and western sometimes.'

'A girl after my own heart,' he teased. 'We'll have to see if there are any concerts in the area we can attend. Alex took me to some when I was little, I remember. Maybe if your mother agrees, we could make up a foursome.'

'That would be nice. I haven't been to a live concert for a long time.'

'What are the young men of Ravenstone thinking about? I can't believe you haven't got them queuing up to take you out. No one special left behind nursing a broken heart? What was the young man's name — Nigel, wasn't it?'

'No,' she replied quietly, recalling her

last confrontation with Nigel. What had he called her? Stand-offish, which she had interpreted as meaning frigid? 'Nigel is an old school friend, that's all.'

Lexie twiddled the engagement ring round and round absentmindedly, trying to decide what she really thought of Jake, especially in this more pleasant teasing mood. Since Camilla was staying until after Christmas, the charade had to continue, and in some ways she felt relieved. She was enjoying her new position deputising for Jake too. At first it had been a bit daunting, but now she relished it and wished it could become a permanent position, although she realised that could never be.

Jake looked much happier and more content heading back to Thornton Grange, and she could understand why, because Thornton Grange was quite a success story. He must only have been a few years older than she was now when he started out, so he had a lot to be proud of. It was no mean achievement.

What would she do when their association was over? Somehow she didn't wish to dwell on that. For the moment, she was gaining valuable experience, and Jake had promised her a reference when she left which should stand her in good stead.

Dinner was over by the time they arrived back at the hotel, so they made do with a snack which Lexie put together from the contents of the fridge. They ate companionably from trays by the fire, both lost in their own private thoughts. It had been a long, tiring day, and both were feeling the effects of so much travelling. Lexie lay back against the cushions, smothering a yawn as the heat from the fire made her drowsy. Her thoughts were erratic, hopping from one subject to another. For some reason, Nigel sprang to mind again. Why him she had no idea, but she remembered how niggled she had been and how uncomfortable she felt being alone with him at Bay View. Yet here she was alone with Jake, feeling quite at home . . . even . . . yes, even sexy.

She was beginning to understand Jake a little; to recognise he had needs like everybody else and he wasn't totally in control of everything as she had believed. His aggressive stance was a cover-up for his unhappy episode with Camilla — that she could understand. She sensed he missed Camilla though, and was probably still in love with her despite the charade they were playing. It was a way of making Camilla jealous enough to fight for him. He wouldn't show his hand too soon — he had learned to his cost that was a mistake; but eventually . . .

She guessed Jake was going to make Camilla wait until New Year before letting her off the hook and telling her his engagement was phoney, by which time, sufficiently cowed, she would accept him on any terms. She could always hope another millionaire would arrive to attract Camilla's attention, but time wasn't on her side, and there was no reason to suppose Jake would wish to make their engagement permanent even if Camilla did go away. He obviously thought she was too young for him.

★   ★   ★

The next morning, Lexie was on her way out of her room when Jake exited the bathroom with a towel draped round his waist. She stared at his bare chest with acute embarrassment. She'd hoped to have made her escape before Jake was up, thinking their next meeting would be much easier to cope with in public.

'I'm sorry,' they said in unison. He tried to side-step her, clearly as embarrassed as she was, but unfortunately as so often happens in these cases, she moved to the same side too. In the confined space they collided, and their chests brushed against each other. An electrifying shock ran through Lexie and she wished the ground would open up. Her cheeks flamed, and with a gasp of unbridled humiliation she ran from the flat. She felt quite dizzy and stood for a moment on the landing outside to recover her composure, wondering how she would ever be able to face him again. Her legs went all rubbery, and she firmly took hold of the banister on her way down to the reception desk, her mind in total confusion. For two pins, she would have carried on walking right out the door. If only she could spend the day on the fells. If only . . .

'Good morning, Miss Prescott.' Sandra looked bright and eager. 'Did you have a pleasant day off?'

'Yes, thank you, Sandra. How were things here? Any problems?' She tried to sound normal, but all the time was terribly self-conscious, as if everyone could hear her heart thudding uncontrollably. She felt they must know what had occurred, which was ridiculous. How could they?

'Nothing we couldn't handle.' Sandra smiled confidently. 'I got Debbie to help me when I got stuck, so we managed between us.'

Lexie continued with her round, greeting all the members of staff she met cheerfully whilst at the same time conscious she would have to face Jake before long, and the prospect terrified her. She was heading for the kitchens when Debbie accosted her.

'Miss Prescott, are you all right? You looked awfully funny just then.'

'I'm fine, thank you, Debbie. Did you want something?'

'Mr Thornton was asking for you. He's waiting in his office. I've just taken in the post.'

Lexie took her time getting to the office. She couldn't make up her mind whether she wanted him to fire her or not. Whether she wanted to leave Thornton Grange or not. All she knew was for a moment last night and this morning, she had so desired Jake that she must have made it abundantly plain to him, and now he would want her to leave. What else could he do? He must have realised their charade couldn't go on, but what would he want to do about it?

'Come in,' Jake called in reply to her timid knock. 'Lexie, come in.'

Fully clothed now, he looked brisk, efficient and business-like. He was frowning at some correspondence almost as if nothing untoward had happened. For a moment she wondered if she had been dreaming.

'I have . . . Are you all right, Lexie?' Jake hurried round the desk. 'Come and sit down. You don't look too grand. For a moment I thought you were going to pass out. Would you like a drink of water, or a cup of coffee maybe?'

'Please.' The next minute was total oblivion. A blackness descended; a spiralling succession of stars flashed by as her legs gave way, and she was falling . . . falling . . .

'Lexie, Lexie.' She heard someone calling her name as if down a long, dark, empty tunnel. She felt cold, lonely and afraid.

'Lexie, are you all right?'

'She's coming round.' Debbie's voice sounded far away.

'Lexie, darling.' That was Jake's voice, rasping with concern. He sounded so sincere, and yet she realised it was because Debbie was present. He really was an exceedingly good actor, she had to give him credit for that. She ought to tell Simon to enlist him for his next production. She wondered what they were going to perform next in the village. *The Taming of the Shrew*, perhaps?

Groggily she opened her eyes. 'I'm all right.' The room was spinning chaotically.

'You had us worried, sweetheart.' Jake was down on his knees leaning over her with a tender, solicitous look on his face. She hazily looked round to see Debbie standing behind him holding a cup of coffee.

'Your colour's coming back now,' she heard her say. 'I thought you didn't look well when we met in the corridor.'

213

Jake turned to her. 'You can return to your duties. I'll see to Lexie now. Thank you for your help, Debbie.'

Lexie tried to get up, conscious she was making a spectacle of herself and not wanting to be alone with Jake.

'Just a minute, take it easy.' Jake put an arm round her neck to support her. 'When you went down, you banged your head on the filing cabinet. I wasn't in time to catch you, unfortunately. When you feel up to it, I'll carry you back to the flat and get Simon to call and take a look at you.'

'There's no need for that. I'll be perfectly all right. I don't know what came over me. I've never fainted in my life. It seemed so warm in here.'

Lexie again tried to get up, only this time Jake took her weight and helped her to the nearest chair. She still felt woozy but tried not to show it.

'Can you think of any reason why you fainted?' Jake asked in an ominously speculative tone. 'You say you've never done it before, so there must be an explanation.' He was watching her colour return, which it did now with a rush.

'No. I know of no reason,' she snapped, angry at what he was insinuating.

'Good, then we'll let Simon diagnose the problem.'

'I'm fine . . . ' Lexie tried to stand, but before she could do so, Jake slid a hand under her legs and picked her up, and despite her protestations carried her back to the flat. Thankfully there were no guests in the reception area to see her making such an exhibition of herself. She was grateful for Jake's assistance though, because she felt definitely wobbly; but whether that was because of his nearness or something else she wasn't certain. Obliged to put her arms round his neck rather than look into his face, she laid her head against his chest and closed her eyes. It felt good. She could smell his particular brand of aftershave, and at one stage her cheek brushed his, sending a tingle of excitement through her. He didn't really think she had lovers, surely — he couldn't! He must know how innocent she was — her kisses must have told him how inexperienced she was with men.

'Stay there until Simon's been. I can't have my staff fainting all over the place,' he admonished her, placing her gently on the settee. 'It's not good for the image we set at Thornton Grange to have members of staff keeling over.'

'Honestly I'm all right, Jake. Please don't bother any more. There's really no need. I have work piling up.'

'Nonsense. If Simon gives you the all-clear, then we'll see . . . or would you rather his father was called? Would it be embarrassing to see Simon?'

'I really don't mind either way. It's totally unnecessary. I'm fine, really I am.'

'Would you like that cup of coffee while we're waiting?' Jake wasn't going to give in.

'Yes please,' she said. 'I'm terribly

thirsty and I still haven't had breakfast.'

'Coffee first then breakfast.'

He brought the coffee, and very shortly afterwards Simon breezed in. 'Now then, my angel, what have you been up to?' His doctor/patient relationship was not at all like the elderly family doctor in Ravenstone. Lexie smiled wanly. 'I go away for a few days and all sorts go on behind my back,' he said with a wry shake of his head.

'I'm fine,' she said. 'There was no need to call you out wasting your time. I'm a bit off colour, that's all.'

'Let me the judge of that. In any case, it isn't often that I get the chance to examine such a beautiful patient. It makes a delightful change from crusty old farmers or howling babies.' He set down his bag and took out his stethoscope. 'I must also offer my congratulations. I've just heard about your engagement. Jake's a lucky guy.'

Fortunately Jake had discreetly left the room, so he didn't witness Lexie's discomfiture. Why couldn't she fall for someone like Simon? she thought wistfully. He would make a wonderful husband, so friendly and likeable. What a pity she didn't feel that way about him.

'How is she?' asked Jake, returning with the coffee pot.

'She'll live,' Simon pronounced in jocular fashion. 'However, she'll need a couple of days in bed. She's got this nasty bug that's going round. Dad's been extra busy while I've been away. It's nothing too serious, unless the rest of your staff go down with it; then you might have problems. Anyone else reported sick?'

'Not so far.'

'I can't stay in bed now,' wailed Lexie. 'It's our busy time.'

'You won't feel much like work for a day or two, I'm afraid. I'll give you some tablets to take which should help, but the best medicine is rest. You've probably been overdoing it, and this is nature's way of telling you to ease up. Too much excitement, maybe?' he said, winking mischievously.

'Thanks, Simon,' Jake said dryly. 'Will you stay for coffee?'

'No, thanks. I have a rash of patients to see, ha ha. You look after your fiancée. Congratulations, by the way. I came across Camilla in the village yesterday evening. She wasn't looking too happy. Now I know why, you sly dog.' He grinned wickedly. 'Lexie will probably want plenty of liquids, preferably non-alcoholic of course, but otherwise tender loving care won't come amiss I'm sure. Don't worry, love, Jake here will look after you, and I know you couldn't be in better hands. Nobody is indispensable, not even me, I find. Dad should have let me know about the epidemic; I could have returned earlier. I'll see myself out. Oh, by the way, I believe I've met your new receptionist before. Sandra isn't it? Sandra Morris. I must go and renew our acquaintance.' He loped off in his usual inimitable style.

Jake brought Lexie a tray with fruit

juice, a boiled egg and toast cut up into soldiers. 'Tuck into that and then back to bed, OK?'

It was late afternoon when she awoke. Someone had been to close the curtains, and the prescription was on the bedside table along with a glass of water and a flask of coffee. Her head felt thick and her throat as dry as the Sahara desert. What a time to be ill, she thought miserably. Just when she wanted to make a good impression. She had probably blown any chance of getting him to see her as more than a step-sister now. Catching sight of herself in the dressing-table mirror only reinforced her prospects. Compared to the likes of Camilla, she looked like a pathetic lovesick schoolgirl.

After a while, she staggered to the bathroom, feeling slightly disoriented. If anything, she felt worse than ever; but instead of returning to bed, she lay on the settee nursing Sebastian. She hoped to pull herself together sufficiently to get dressed before Jake returned but gradually dozed off. It was the key in the lock that woke her. She stirred and stretched as the cat jumped down on hearing his master's voice.

'Hello there,' Jake said. 'How are you feeling?'

'Oh, Jake. I'm feeling so lethargic,' she muttered sleepily. She felt as if her legs were made of cotton wool, and her head was muzzy.

Jake threw his jacket on to a chair. 'Do you think you can you manage to eat something?'

'I dare say I could manage an odd morsel,' she replied with a grin.

He laughed and began rolling up his sleeves. 'Glad to see it hasn't affected your appetite. We can't have you fading away before Alex and Jessica get in.'

'Have you heard when they're arriving?' she asked, trying to smother a great big yawn.

'Yes, just this morning. That was something I wanted to tell you before you blacked out. They should arrive back in England at the end of next week. You haven't read your mail, I take it?'

'No I haven't.' She suddenly remembered stuffing it in her pocket when Sandra handed it to her earlier because she was still in a state of confusion after her encounter with Jake.

'How about an omelette with mushrooms and a salad. Does that sound all right, madam?'

'That would be lovely, but I feel such a fraud lying here leaving it all to you. I shall be forever in your debt.'

'Think nothing of it. I enjoy cooking, as a matter of fact, although I don't get much opportunity.'

He left her to go and prepare the meal while she lay back with a sigh of repletion. This must be heaven. She couldn't remember when she'd last had a lazy day with a feeling of such detachment. Nothing else mattered anymore. Everything she wanted or needed was here in the flat, especially now Jake was home and in a genial mood. Her mind finally admitted defeat. Far from wanting to get away from Jake, she wanted to get closer. She was in love with him. She knew it was insane and totally incomprehensible, but it was true — she loved him. She didn't know how she was going to cope with her crazy feelings, but for the moment she was happy to be there in his flat alone with him. She smiled inwardly, wondering what he would think if he knew. Perhaps he did, but was used to women falling in love with him, so one more scalp to add to his tally made little difference.

They ate their meal, and afterwards she found she couldn't keep her eyes open. The tablets must be making her dopey, she thought hazily. She didn't remember sliding sideways, but woke a short time later to discover herself captive in Jake's arms and could hear his heart beating like a metronome — smooth and rhythmical. She gazed at his face mellowed in sleep, wanting to gently lift the lock of hair back off his forehead. Such a high forehead and prominent cheekbones, thick bushy eyebrows and exceptionally long lashes — she'd never noticed before. It was such an interesting face. Suddenly she realised he'd woken up and was staring right back at her, his eyes soft and gentle. She blushed, but made no attempt to escape his clutches; she didn't want to break the spell.

'That was the best sleep I've had for a long time,' he murmured huskily. 'You are a very restful person to have around, Lexie.'

'I'm sorry, did I wake you?' It was with great regret that she extricated herself.

'I don't know, but in any case I'll have to stir myself. I have to go out, unfortunately.' He stood up, stretched and yawned. 'Pity really, because I don't feel too bright. I wouldn't have minded a night in for a change.'

Jake drove out of the car park wondering if Lexie knew exactly what she was doing. At times she appeared naïvely innocent, but it could all be an act. Why didn't he accept her for what she was — a simple, charming young woman who was managing to cope with what life threw her way? He would like to believe her. He would like their relationship to develop further; dammit, he was in love with her. He slammed the palm of his hand against the steering wheel with frustration. The prospect was totally irrational. So why was he driving about the countryside instead of sharing his own fireside with her? He had manufactured an excuse because those eyes bewitched him. At least he was clear-headed enough to realise that!

Lexie didn't hear him return as the tablets knocked her out, but it was a disturbed restless sleep from which she woke several times to find the bedcovers all awry. She remembered dreaming about Simon. He was standing over her telling her she must stay in bed and she kept saying, 'No Simon, no I can't, I can't.' Then he vanished to be replaced by Jake. He sat beside her soothingly, patting her forehead with a damp cloth. He kissed her gently, as he would a small child, and she heard him sigh — a deep, sad sigh. She didn't like to think of him being so sad, so she murmured she loved him over and over again. She told him she never ever wanted to leave Thornton Grange. She wanted to reassure him of her love, but still he sighed.

The face cloth was on the bedside table when she woke. Her cheeks were on fire, her throat parched, and yet she was shivering almost uncontrollably. She wondered how much had been a dream and how much reality as she restored order to the bedcovers. She was considering making a move when Jake tapped on the door and entered.

'Morning, Lexie.' He handed her a large glass of orange juice. She noticed he was still in his dressing gown as if he hadn't been up very long.

'You look tired. I'm sorry, I disturbed you didn't I?'

'It's all part of the Thornton Grange

226

motto. Twenty-four-hour service. We never close.' He half smiled, but it looked forced. 'You're looking better this morning.'

She felt a wreck. 'Thank you for what you did during the night. I thought I'd been dreaming.'

'You were delirious and feverish, but at least it was getting out of your system. Take it easy today. I shall be away on business most of the day, but Sandra's coping all right so there's no need to worry.'

Lexie settled back against the pillows, her mind in turmoil. How much had she said out loud? Had she really told Jake she loved him? Was that why he looked grim this morning? Was he regretting the situation they had got themselves into? Had she made a complete fool of herself?

For the rest of the day, she pottered about in her dressing gown listening to music, nursing the cat and reading some of Jake's books. The maid came during the morning to tidy, and more logs arrived for the fire. Debbie brought her a light lunch and stayed for a few minutes chatting. During the afternoon she dozed for a while on the settee, but woke feeling so much better that she decided to have a shower and change into a pair of slacks and a blouse. Maybe she could still set her stall out to compete with Camilla. She had the advantage of wearing Jake's ring and seeing him daily. It would be worth a try, she thought, and at the moment she had nothing to lose. She was about to prepare the table for a meal when Jake returned looking exhausted, but he brightened up considerably when he saw her.

'You're obviously feeling better.'

'Yes, much better thanks; but you look about whacked. Why don't you go and have a shower while I prepare a meal.'

He dropped his briefcase on the settee and wearily loosened his tie. 'If you're quite sure you feel up to it, that sounds marvellous. I was going to suggest having something sent up.'

Lexie suddenly felt wonderful. She explored the fridge and cupboards for ingredients and found some juicy steaks along with a variety of prepared vegetables. She popped some potatoes into the microwave and heated up the vegetables while the grill was made ready for the steaks. If she'd thought earlier, she could have made a more exotic sweet, but had to settle for ice cream topped with fruit. It wasn't exactly cordon bleu cooking, but at least they were alone. Camilla hadn't been to the flat as far as she knew; at least she hadn't on this trip.

Lexie enjoyed herself in the small kitchen and arranged the lounge table attractively. She would like to have used some candles she found in the kitchen cupboard but felt that would look too intimate, so settled for twisting the serviettes. Everything was almost ready when Jake reappeared, dressed casually with his hair still damp from the shower and his curls tight and springy. The scene was delightfully cosy, with the table set for two and the fire casting shadows about the room. She'd only switched on a small table lamp, which shed a gentle glow. She thought it was quite a romantic setting, but Jake appeared not to notice.

'Debbie says everything's all right downstairs,' she said. 'She told me Sandra's taken over the reception duties extremely well.'

Jake nodded. 'She's fitted in OK. I gather she was delighted to renew her acquaintance with Simon.'

He gave her an arched look but she merely nodded back. After that, he barely spoke throughout the rest of the meal, making her wonder whether he was coming down with the bug too. They spent a tranquil evening together lounging and listening to music. Jake remained exceptionally reserved, reading correspondence and more or less ignoring Lexie, so she tried to take her cue from him. At least he had stayed in the flat and not gone seeking Camilla's company, for which she was grateful; but all the same, Lexie would have liked some sign he wasn't oblivious to her. She tried making conversation, but it was obvious he wasn't in a sociable mood and wished to be left alone. She retired to bed early feeling a little miffed at his attitude, but put it down to him being disturbed the previous night. She would have to keep trying.

# 9

Tom and Madge Trufitt arrived at the hotel one evening accompanied by their daughter and another elderly couple. It was the first time Lexie had met them, and she found them to be charming people — much nicer than she had expected.

'Jake tells me that you're Alex Thornton's daughter?' said Joe Trufitt, vigorously shaking her hand.

'Yes, I'm expecting him and my mother at any moment.'

'I know. I'm looking forward to meeting them again. He's an interesting chap, your father. Knows his stuff, too.'

'I gather the flight was late arriving,' Jake said, 'but they should be here before long. Shall we go into the bar to wait for them?'

It was to be a sort of welcome home which should have been a happy occasion, but Lexie was beginning to feel anxious. She was looking forward to seeing them of course, but she couldn't decide how best to tell them about her phoney engagement. It would be tricky mentioning it in front of the Trufitts, but if she didn't tell them straightaway it would look very strange. She had wanted to discuss it with Jake, but there didn't seem to be the right time in which to do so.

'Here they are,' declared Jake, and a cheer went up. Alex and Jessica appeared looking suntanned and radiantly happy. In the following few minutes, it seemed everybody was congratulating everyone else. Lexie found herself hugged first by her father and then her mother.

'We're so happy to hear about your engagement, darling,' Jessica chuckled delightedly. 'Jake will make you a wonderful husband. We couldn't be happier.'

Lexie glanced at Jake, who was deep in conversation with Alex and Joe, but had obviously heard her mother's observation. He grinned across and winked, leaving Lexie in a desperate quandary.

'We were wondering if you'd want to have your name changed legally to Thornton, but this is a far better way,' her mother continued. 'We're both thrilled at how well everything has turned out. It's been quite a year, hasn't it?'

Lexie was now horrified. She couldn't refute the engagement, especially since Camilla and Madge Trufitt were taking part in the general conversation and overheard everything.

'It just happened,' Lexie murmured, trying to look suitably happy, but it was quite an effort and Jake was no help. He was leaving her to cope alone, so she floundered awkwardly. He might have mentioned he'd informed her parents. That way she would have been better prepared. Unfortunately, she found herself seated next to Camilla. 'What line of work are you in?' she asked her in desperation as a way of changing the subject.

'I don't work,' Camilla replied disdainfully. 'I don't need to. Work is for drudges.'

Lexie bit her tongue. She turned to Madge sitting opposite and tried to draw her into the conversation. 'I gather you live at the beautiful house across the lake? I've often admired it. It must have some wonderful views. Mother, you should see it. It has the most marvellous garden stretching right down to the water. And the rhododendron bushes, they're magnificent. I'll bet they're a real picture when they're in bloom.'

Madge and her mother struck up a conversation and soon became engrossed in a debate on the merits of shrubs versus flowerbeds. Lexie was pleased, but it left her and Camilla alone with nothing to say to each other. The men were in a huddle of their own and sounded like they were discussing business. Camilla looked intensely angry because for once Jake was ignoring her. She tried several times to attract his attention, but Jake avoided her plaintive gestures. Lexie felt the atmosphere was volatile and wondered what Camilla would do if nobody took any notice of her. She didn't feel it was up to her to be sociable toward her. She had been snubbed once and wouldn't go out of her way for a repetition, but she could see Camilla seething with annoyance. She was greatly relieved when Sandra needed some assistance and she was called to the reception desk. It got her out of the way for a few minutes in which she could compose herself before returning to the party and sitting beside her mother well away from Camilla.

The evening dragged on, with Lexie on tenterhooks the whole time. She could have murdered Jake for not warning her in advance, even though it had actually helped the situation. Fortunately her parents were tired with all the travelling and wanted an early night, so eventually the party broke up — and none too soon, as far as Lexie was concerned.

'Jake, I can't go on with this charade. You saw how pleased my mother was. What's she going to think when we tell them it's phoney?' Lexie had sat up waiting for him. It had been a long wait too, but she felt she had to convince him it was a mistake. She had to explain at least to her parents exactly what the position was.

'I thought we agreed all this,' Jake said wearily. 'We can't suddenly change it now. After all, it won't be for much longer.'

'I know, but . . . '

'Go to bed, Lexie,' he said irritably. 'Nothing's changed.'

'I didn't . . . ' She couldn't go on. She wished she had never agreed to the silly arrangement. The fact Jake was supposed to be no longer available didn't appear to make the slightest difference as far as Camilla was concerned.

'I hate you!' she cried and ran from the room. Now her parents were back and she had seen for herself their reaction, she realised how stupid she had been to accept the situation. She should have known how delighted they would be to have Jake as a son-in-law. How could she have been so dim-witted?

★   ★   ★

In the following days, they were barely civil to each other. Jake was acting distinctly cool except in public, where he still managed to keep up the masquerade. Lexie noticed he kept himself extraordinarily busy and refrained from being in the flat for much of the time, especially when he knew she was likely to be there. Camilla had taken to spending a good deal more time at the hotel, and that angered her intensely. Whenever Lexie felt there was an opportunity to restore some sort of camaraderie with Jake, Camilla would appear and drag him away with some feeble excuse. Camilla hadn't given up on Jake, that was obvious and there seemed to be nothing Lexie could do to win him over.

'What shall we do about Camilla?' she asked him one day when their paths crossed for once. 'She spends so much time here even though she's not a resident.'

'What do you mean?' he asked grumpily.

'Do we send her a bill at the end of the week? She uses the facilities as if she owns the place, and I've not seen her pay for a single meal. All she ever does is complain about the service she receives.' She would like to have added she was also behaving outrageously by monopolising Jake. Had he forgotten he was supposed to be engaged to her, not Camilla?

'She's here as my guest,' Jake growled. 'So don't go causing trouble.

Just ignore her.'

Lexie bit back an angry retort and stalked out. She was finding it extremely hard to keep her cool with Jake in such a strange mood. He seemed more touchy and unpredictable than ever. As for Camilla, she was almost deliberately provocative.

'It'll never last. Jake's trying to please your father. Surely you must realise you're not in his league,' Camilla taunted her one day when they were unfortunate enough to be alone in the powder room together.

'Think what you like,' Lexie replied with a withering look, 'but I'm the one wearing his ring.'

'Huh, Jake is too chivalrous by half. If you had any sense, you'd see he feels trapped and doesn't know how to get out of it. He loves me, he always has, and you must be blind if you can't see it.'

Tears smarted Lexie's eyes but she blinked them away. 'You had your opportunity and you botched it, so why don't you go back to where you came from and leave Jake alone,' she said, and quickly left the room.

★　★　★

The preparations for Christmas were well underway. Jake and Lexie were so busy that their paths rarely crossed, Jake being involved mostly in other business matters and leaving Lexie to cope with the running of the hotel. Camilla visited almost daily but Lexie went out of her way to avoid greeting her. She did, however, feel deeply aggrieved to see Jake enjoying, even seeking out Camilla's company. One day they were laughing together in the bar and Lexie saw red. It was the last straw. She was convinced they were sharing a joke at her expense, having seen the supercilious look Camilla flashed in her direction. She flounced back to the flat and slammed the door as hard she could, annoyed with herself as much as anything for being jealous of

Camilla. What a tangle, she thought. She loved Jake, but he seemed oblivious to the fact; he only had eyes for Camilla. And yet he hadn't asked for an end to their phoney engagement.

'I thought I saw you disappearing up here. Are you all right?' Jake strode in and began rummaging though papers in the writing desk.

'Yes, thank you, I'm fine. Don't let me detain you from your guest!' she snapped.

'It was an impressive performance you gave.' He grinned. 'You really did look jealous.' He left the flat whistling cheerfully.

'Oh, men!' declared Lexie in frustration. She had to do something to rid herself of her animosity; she was in no state to deal with the guests like this. Realising it had been quite some time since she had been out walking — she had been so busy about the hotel preparing for Christmas she hadn't taken much time off — she decided now she would put on her boots and go. *See if I care what Jake and the Lady Camilla get up to.*

Camilla made her sick, swanning around in her furs making eyes at any newcomer to the hotel when Jake wasn't looking. She did for an instant consider asking Alex if he would care to accompany her, but in the event decided not to. She wasn't really fit company for anyone; it would be better if she went alone. Leaving by way of the fire escape, she set off at a brisk pace down through the village, not altogether sure where she was heading; but it didn't really matter. The weather was cold and slightly misty, but the ground was reasonable underfoot.

She tramped along, ridding herself of all the anger and jealousy and muttering to herself, oblivious to the strange looks she received from passers-by. Normally she would have greeted everybody cheerily, but today she was in a private world of her own as she tried to rationalise her feelings toward Jake. She wasn't exactly planning to go anywhere specifically, she was just walking, so it was by chance she found herself on an unknown path.

She was so deep in thought that she hadn't realised how far she had walked until she stopped to catch her breath once clear of the trees. She had covered some distance. Thornton Grange, impressively floodlit on the far side of the lake, looked dramatically enchanting with its tall Christmas tree lit up outside, and she thought about how she was going to miss it all when she had to leave. She didn't want to go, but on the other hand she couldn't bear to stay if Jake didn't love her and worse still married Camilla.

Lexie sighed. She had grown to love this wonderful, peaceful place. It wasn't just the scenery, it was the people she worked with too. It was going to be hard walking away from it all. She would also miss Jake more than she cared to admit. She couldn't understand him, but that was neither here nor there. One minute he was so wonderful — loving even, and then he became cold and aggressive for no apparent reason.

With a despairing sigh, she set off again, finding a path to take her back slightly higher up than her usual one. It would be dark long before she reached the hotel, she realised, and she had walked out without letting anyone know where she was going. That was one thing Jake had impressed upon her right from the start, never to go walking about the hills without leaving word of her proposed route in case they needed to call out the mountain rescue team. Simon had said the same thing. They both seemed to think it vitally important.

Well she didn't need rescuing; she knew exactly where she was and the hotel was not far away. It would do Jake good to worry about her for a change and perhaps take his mind off Camilla. She dawdled for a while, wondering what would happen if she stayed out all night. What if she got herself lost

— would Jake come looking for her, and like the gallant hero in romantic novels discover he was desperately in love with her? They would marry and live happily ever after like all good fairy tales. The thought was enough to make her smile. He would more than likely alert her parents, and she knew she couldn't let that happen. She didn't want them upset. It spurred her into lengthening her stride, anxious now about the amount of time she had been away. The air was becoming noticeably colder and she pulled her hood up, pushing her hair inside clumsily with gloved hands. Perhaps snow was on the way, she thought. It would transform the scene into something magical, and a white Christmas would be wonderful. She couldn't ever remember a white Christmas, and to have one here at this time would be memorable.

Finally the trees thinned out, but the path seemed to keep on meandering upwards, which surprised her as she had expected it to join the lower path back down to the track behind the hotel. But what horrified her was the mist that had descended so she couldn't see the valley bottom. It was a thick, wet, murky blanket covering the whole of the valley. It drifted into the trees like smoke from a garden bonfire, blanking out her points of reference.

She paused and listened, but could only vaguely hear the sounds of motor vehicles on the road which ran through the valley bottom alongside the lake. Should she stay with the original path, or strike out on her own heading down the hillside? Neither route appealed, since she was on unknown territory. The only other alternative was to turn back; but that would mean a long, long trek, and surely it couldn't be so arduous finding her way down through the fields. If the sheep could find a way, it couldn't be so difficult. The one thing that stuck in her mind was that there was an old abandoned slate quarry in the area with steep shale slopes. She wouldn't want to come across that in the gloom.

She felt decidedly cold as she struck off in the direction she anticipated the hotel to be. The toes of her right foot were extremely sore, so she didn't feel like retracing her steps, nor did she relish the idea of climbing up to the top of the hill where she might find an alternative route down. It was eerie being out on the fells alone, and she hummed quietly to keep her spirits up, wondering if she had been missed already. It was one thing to read in books about being lost in the hills, which made it sound exciting; but experiencing it for real was something else. Would Jake be annoyed or upset when he realised she was missing? What if she couldn't find a way down? What if she did have to stay out all night, or at least until the mist lifted? But it might remain for days. That thought terrified her, so she quickened her stride, trying to keep the weight off her right foot as much as possible. In Ravenstone she could have found her way through the thickest fog, but this was quite different.

Everywhere looked totally alien. She came to a stone wall topped with barbed wire which she followed for a time hoping to find an opening, but eventually gave up and scrambled over, tearing her jacket in the process. By now she was well and truly frightened and wishing she had never set off. Stumbling over a stone, she cursed again as she ended up slithering down a grassy bank, finally coming to rest just in time to stop herself from falling head first into a stream. She listened but could hear nothing — nothing at all except her own heavy breathing. She felt like bawling her eyes out.

As she was wearily getting to her feet, she thought she heard something — a faint noise. Was it a sheep? Then she saw lights. They were only dim and a little way away, but at least it meant civilisation. She began hobbling down the hillside, the lights urging her on. At least she wouldn't have to spend the night out after all. What would she not give for a hot bath!

As quickly as she could, she followed the stream until she came out on a cart track. A short way down was a farmhouse with lights showing through the uncurtained windows. She breathed a sigh of relief. With luck, the farmer could direct her to the village, or better still, the hotel; and maybe he had transport. She had no money on her, but she could reimburse him when they got to the hotel.

She was a few yards from the farm gate when a car emerged. Slowly at first, but to Lexie it was the last straw. If the driver didn't see her, she knew she would give up. She couldn't walk another step. She waved and shouted, and someone from the house came to have a word with the driver, giving Lexie time to stagger those last few precious yards.

'Simon, am I glad to see you,' she cried, flopping against the bonnet.

'What on earth are you doing out here, Lexie?' he asked, getting out of the car.

She grimaced. 'I went for a walk and it turned out to be far longer than I anticipated.'

Simon shook his head. 'You shouldn't be out on your own in this weather. The mist is closing in. Hop in I'll give you lift back. You look all in.'

'Thanks. I got lost and was having visions of staying out all night until I saw the lights.' Lexie shuffled into the passenger seat with a contented sigh. The warmth and comfort of the car interior were more than welcome.

'Here, wrap this rug round you. We don't want you coming down with pneumonia. Jake will be wondering where the devil you've got to.'

Lexie pulled a face. 'I shouldn't think so,' she murmured. 'He has other things on his mind. Anyway, I only came out for a stroll to clear my head. I didn't intend walking so far.'

Simon engaged a gear and the car

rolled slowly down the track. It was a twisty road and needed his whole attention, as the mist was getting thicker by the minute.

'You shouldn't take such chances with these hills, you know,' he said. 'The mist comes down quite quickly at times and even an experienced walker can get lost. You don't want to be ill at Christmas now, do you? You should have got Jake or someone to come with you if you felt like a breather. Jake knows these hills better than most.'

'Jake was otherwise engaged,' she muttered, fiddling with the seat belt. 'It was fine when I set off, but I lost track of time.'

'Everything all right between you?' he asked, glancing across at her.

'Yes, of course. Why shouldn't it be?'

'No reason, only . . . I guess this is your busy time, but after the festivities you need a holiday — doctor's orders.'

She smiled. 'I'm okay, honestly. Just cold, a little tired, and rather footsore.'

Simon dropped her off outside the

hotel, suggesting she get into a hot bath and have an early night. As she stumbled across the car park, she saw Jake coming towards her, concern on his face.

'Where have you been? I've been looking all over for you. I was about to send out a search party.'

'Out,' she said, and carried on walking. She was in no mood to deal with him just then, but he caught her by the arm.

'Why didn't you leave word to say where you were going? And how come you were in Simon Jackson's car?'

'I didn't *know* where I was going. I needed to get away for a while. Simon happened to come by, and I was tired, so he gave me a lift. Now if you don't mind, my feet hurt and I need a bath.'

'What's wrong?'

'Nothing's wrong,' she said wearily. 'I needed time to myself, that's all.' She pulled her arm free. 'You don't own me, Jake, and I do have feelings. I can't take much more of this.'

He looked put out at her reply. 'I told you to leave word when you went walkabout. I don't like the idea of you being out alone around here. You don't know the area. Anything could happen to you.'

'I wanted to escape!' she shouted. 'You and your precious Camilla! I'm sick of it all! I want to be left alone.' Lexie was close to tears. She turned and ran to the fire escape. 'Just leave me alone.' She didn't wait to see if he would follow.

The bath was sheer bliss. She pampered herself with plenty of scented bath oils and lay back reflectively. Had he really been concerned? If so, was it concern for her safety, or for his own reputation? Or was it because he'd been distracted from his pursuit of Camilla?

Her sore feet were blistered and would be uncomfortable for a day or two, she surmised as she contemplated what to wear that evening. She had to try to recover her composure. She couldn't let her parents see her upset.

They were still basking in their newfound love for each other and clearly delighted Jake and Lexie were supposedly soon to follow suit. She couldn't spoil things for them before Christmas. Maybe after the festivities? Whatever Jake thought, whatever promise she had made, she knew she could not continue like this for much longer.

Jake knocking on the door intruded into her daydream. She hadn't realised how long she had spent luxuriating there. 'Lexie, are you in there?' he called.

'I'll be out in a minute.' Stepping out of the bath, she draped herself in a towel. Even Jake's presence in the flat couldn't persuade her to put on her discarded soiled clothes.

He was leaning nonchalantly against the wall outside the door. 'Have you recovered your temper yet?' he asked when she appeared.

'There was nothing wrong with my temper. I don't like being interrogated like a schoolgirl or made fun of behind my back.'

'I suppose walking out without telling anyone where you were going sounded like a great idea to you, did it?'

'I didn't mean to walk so far. I just walked. I was in sight of the hotel most of the time.' She didn't want to tell him she had got lost and had been extremely frightened by her ordeal.

'Do you know how long you were out there? Debbie saw you in the car park heading for the village over three hours ago.'

'I'm sorry. I didn't realise you would even notice I'd gone. You seemed to have plenty of other more important things on your mind than worrying about me. Camilla, perhaps?'

'Forget about her. Did you even consider you were worrying the life out of me?'

'I didn't do it on purpose. I lost track of time. I knew exactly where I was all the way,' she lied.

'You might have done, but it would

have been useful if I'd had that knowledge too.' He sighed. 'Anyway, if you're up to it after everything that's happened, I need you to get into your acting role for dinner.'

Lexie agreed, hoping it would get her mind off things, though she was no longer comfortable doing this and knew she would have to tell him soon. She spent a little while teasing her hair into something approaching an acceptable style and then had trouble finding footwear which was anything like comfortable. She eventually managed with some low-heeled mules, and with a shrug of her shoulders went down to dinner.

# 10

It was lovely having her parents back, but unfortunately her mother kept chatting blithely about how splendid it was going to be having them living in the top flat at Bay View. Lexie had to distract her the best way she could. If only she really was going to live there, how marvellous it would be. Come the New Year, she would have to start looking for another job. It was a pity, but there was no way she could stay in the Lake District. It was plain Jake did not love her. What was it women like Camilla had that attracted men? she wondered. The only way she was going to get through the next two weeks was to immerse herself in work and try not to think about the future too much.

Since the staff could only use the swimming pool late at night, she had taken to having a swim each evening before retiring. She enjoyed the exercise and found pleasure in having the pool to herself; it was rare anybody else was there so late. One evening, however, Jake appeared at the poolside, taking her completely by surprise.

'So this is where you get to, is it?'

'I hope I'm not breaking any house rules.'

'No of course not. Simon's in the bar. I thought he might be looking for you.'

'Simon doesn't run after other men's women. He believes I'm engaged to you, don't forget.' She heaved herself out of the pool and sat wringing the water out of her hair. 'I expect he's waiting for Sandra to come off duty.'

'I suppose in the circumstances you can't wait to come clean about our arrangement, can you?' Jake said, handing her a towel.

'Of course not. I told you, I don't like deception. More specifically, I don't like deceiving my parents. Mum keeps on about how wonderful it's all going to be. How do you think that makes me feel?'

'I'm sorry, but it won't be for much longer,' he said, walking away.

Jake cursed under his breath as he strode out of the front door. Why hadn't he taken the opportunity to tell her how he felt about her? He wished he knew how she would react if he did. He was wary of making a fool of himself again. He could not fathom her extraordinary co-operation. Was it just her nature, or did it indicate something more? She had looked like a beautiful nymph in her bathing costume, and yet she seemed totally unconscious of the effect she was having on him. Every time they were alone together, he felt the urge to tell her exactly how he felt, but something held him back. She made light of Simon Jackson's attraction to Sandra, but he realised how hurt she must feel, and he wanted to help ease the pain but didn't know how. He took a turn round the garden and waited until he saw the light go on in her bedroom before returning. Not much longer, he sighed. Soon everything would be resolved one way or another — they would have to be if he was to keep his sanity.

Lexie went to get dry, feeling even more dejected than ever. Jake's appearance by the pool had ruined the desired effect, and she returned to the flat tense and irritable. She slumped onto the hearth-rug in front of the fire to dry her hair. 'At least you seem to love me,' she murmured as Sebastian nuzzled up against her, purring loudly. 'Whatever does your boss see in her?' she asked despondently. 'If only you could talk, perhaps you could give me a few tips. After all, he loves you, doesn't he? Maybe he only likes redheads. Perhaps I should dye my hair.' Picking him up, she went to sit on the settee. Stroking the cat was very therapeutic, and she was soon very sleepy.

★ ★ ★

On Christmas Eve, the hotel was bustling with activity. It had been a particularly busy day with all sorts of problems to be overcome, from a near disaster in the kitchen to a shortage of bed linen. Eventually all was satisfactorily solved, and after a reviving shower, Lexie slipped into a blue taffeta dress ready to greet the guests at the pre-dinner cocktail party. She hoped Jake would approve, but recently she felt she could have gone around in sackcloth for all the notice he took. She went to a great deal of trouble fixing her hair into an elaborate style. It was now quite long, and she had set it on large rollers to give it some lift.

A final check in the wardrobe mirror brought a smile to her reflection, her morale lifted by pleasure with the result. Sandra had told her Simon was attending tonight, and there were several guests who were definitely interesting. She considered retaliating if Jake made a play for Camilla, but it wouldn't be fair on the guests. She still seethed with anger at the way Camilla shamelessly hung around him. She left the flat determined to enjoy herself; there was only another week to go. *Surely I can manage to last that long*, she mused. But one more week and then what?

The evening proved to be great fun. The guests were in high spirits, ready to have a good time at all costs, and Lexie found herself fending off several amorous young men who had perhaps overindulged at the bar. It amused her to find Jake hovering as a deterrent to their advances, causing Camilla to glare malevolently at her. Camilla wasn't used to being ignored. Lexie wondered if they'd had words, since they didn't look too happy with each other.

Jake spent a good deal of time looking after the guests and making everyone welcome, especially those on their own. He was the perfect host. The festivities went on well into the early hours of Christmas morning, by which time Lexie felt drained. She knew the staff had worked magnificently; they had certainly earned their Christmas bonuses. Returning to the flat, she flopped down on the sofa and kicked off her shoes. Her nerves were on edge. If anything, the charade had been easier tonight. In such an atmosphere of frivolity, she could genuinely feel love towards Jake, and he in turn had looked more amenable tonight, even protective. He'd complimented her on her dress when they were alone, which had made her feel exhilarated because he sounded sincere. It was only a small token, but it was very welcome. That, plus the fact Camilla didn't appear to have the Christmas spirit, gave her some relief.

'Fancy a nightcap?' Jake asked, emerging from the bathroom in his towelling robe. 'Someone spilt their drink down me. I hope it doesn't stain the shirt; it was one of my favourites.'

'Have you put it in to soak?'

He nodded. 'Christmas is fun but exhausting, isn't it? I expect this is quite a change from what you're used to. It's a pity it didn't snow. It was forecast, although it doesn't often snow down in the village this early in the winter.' He poured them both a drink and handed her a present at the same time wrapped in attractive paper and festive ribbons. 'I know that tomorrow, or rather later today, will be pretty hectic, so maybe you ought to have this now. Happy Christmas, Lexie. You're doing a splendid job. You're definitely an asset to have around the place.'

'Oh,' she said gingerly, untying the fancy bow. She had been wondering what he would do about her Christmas present. She thought maybe he would leave it under the tree with the rest of the staff presents which she had helped organise. Inside the luxury wrapping paper was a long black leather case. She hardly dared to open it because she knew whatever it contained would be expensive. The case alone with its conspicuous gold lettering gave it away. She could sense him watching as she teased it open.

'It's beautiful,' she gasped. Inside was the most magnificent emerald necklace she had ever seen. Fingering the glittering stones, she looked up at him. 'But you shouldn't have. It must have cost a small fortune. I can't possibly accept it.' She just knew they were real gems.

He shrugged his shoulders and grinned. 'We're engaged, remember? It's expected.'

'We both know that's an act,' she said. 'There was no need to spend so much money on a present for me.' She hastily stood up and pushed the box back at him, tears stinging her eyes. His cynicism upset her more than she could cope with. The next thing to spring to mind was that the jewels had probably been bought for Camilla. They were definitely the sort of present she would expect. She didn't want Camilla's cast-offs. She would have been happier with a simple paperback if he'd chosen it specially for her.

He was by her side in a flash. 'Lexie, look at me,' he said in a tender tone. He took her chin in his hand. She nibbled her bottom lip. His nearness made her jumpy. On the dance floor it wasn't a problem, but here alone in the flat together she could feel her head spin. Was he going to kiss her? She blinked.

'I chose the necklace because those stones reminded me of your beautiful green eyes. They really are most fascinating. I hoped you'd like it too. I thought it would complement the ring. Don't cry, Lexie. Please don't cry. I really do appreciate all you've done. I'm grateful. I know how difficult it's been for you. Camilla's proved to be more of a troublemaker than I anticipated, but it won't be for much longer, I promise you.' He wanted to say something else — something which would make it easier, but he couldn't quite find the words.

Lexie nodded resignedly and reached out for the present she had put on the side table for him, glad now she had not left it downstairs with the rest. Obviously he felt Camilla was becoming sufficiently jealous; the charade was working to his satisfaction at least. This was how he showed his gratitude — the payoff. Now she understood.

'Thank you,' she said quietly. 'I'll treasure it always. I hope you like the present I bought for you.' It had taken a great deal of thought before she had finally decided to buy him a wine-coloured sweater and a Mozart CD.

He opened it immediately and seemed genuinely pleased. 'Thank you, Lexie. It was most thoughtful of you. You have such excellent taste — I believe I've already told you so.'

'I hope it fits,' she said shyly, unexpectedly finding herself in his arms. Her face was pressed against his chest and she heard his heart beating like a tomtom. She looked up in time to see a strange fleeting expression pass over his face before his mouth descended. The kiss was gentle yet seductive — but tantalising, leaving her unfulfilled and irrationally wanting to prolong it.

'Merry Christmas, sweetheart,' he whispered almost inaudibly. 'Merry Christmas.' It had been a long time since he'd kissed her — properly kissed her — not just the odd peck on the cheek for public consumption.

She wished she *was* his sweetheart; she wished he would kiss her again and again. She could make him forget Camilla if he gave her a chance. Gently he released her, and feeling over-whelmed, she ran from the room shouting, 'Merry Christmas, Jake.'

She slumped against the bedroom door with her hands over her face, shuddering with emotion. She didn't know how much longer she could go on like this. It felt in a way as if he was teasing her. She knew he wanted to make Camilla jealous and had been prepared to help, but not at such a price. She loved him desperately and couldn't help showing it, despite his cool manner towards her of late.

She hardly slept a wink as she relentlessly thought about the New Year, wondering how Jake was going to explain their inevitable breakup. Would he expect some sort of argument to develop in which she threw him back his ring? Then he could openly announce he and Camilla were getting married. She wouldn't do it! It wouldn't be fair to ask it of her.

The next morning she had to try extra hard to get into the festive mood. It seemed to be an interminably long day. Finally she could keep going no longer and escaped to the privacy of her room. She had kept out of Jake's way as much as possible, trying to appear happy, but underneath she felt thoroughly miserable. She saw her mother looking at her rather anxiously from time to time as if suspecting something was amiss, so she pleaded a headache.

Entertainment for Boxing Day involved a trip on Lake Windermere complete with afternoon tea. The weather didn't look too promising to start with, but by lunch time it had brightened up; and when they set off, the sun was actually shining, if somewhat weakly. The party on board was in exceptional spirits, singing rowdily as they made their way round the lake. That night was party night with a buffet and dance arranged. For many of the guests it was their last night before returning to work, so they were making the most of it. Lexie had decided to wear the green silk dress she had bought in Kendal and the emeralds which Jake had given her for Christmas. They certainly enhanced the dress, but she grimaced at her reflection in the mirror, wondering if perhaps she ought to return them along with the ring when they called off the engagement. She couldn't ever envisage being able wear them on any other occasion she was likely to attend when she became an ordinary working girl again.

She tried to put out of her mind the time when she would have to leave and find herself another job and place to stay. So far she hadn't attempted to find other employment, but she knew she would have to before long. Her savings wouldn't last forever, and she didn't want to have to rely on her parents to keep her. Every time she contemplated the future, she felt a gnawing pain in her stomach. She hated the idea of leaving Thornton Grange and yet at the same time knew she couldn't remain, unless . . . But that was out of the question, it appeared; and she sighed sorrowfully. Ah well. The New Year would soon be upon them.

Her parents were staying to let the New Year in before returning to Ravenstone, and Lexie wondered if she ought to go home with them, but wasn't even sure if she could bring herself to live at Bay View after all that had happened. She would never know when Jake was going to be there visiting. He might even bring Camilla as his wife, she thought, aghast at the prospect.

'You look particularly beautiful tonight,' Jake said, waltzing her round the floor — a duty dance. By all accounts, Camilla had made up with Jake and was once again in favour. 'I was right, those stones do bring out the beauty of your eyes.'

'Thank you,' was all she could say. Compliments were easy to distribute; but whether meant or not, who could tell? He held her so close she could feel his muscular frame through the thin fabric of her dress, the familiar tingle again filling her with shameless desire. If only it could go on and on forever, she thought. With the lights down low and the music gently weaving its magic, she felt as if they were alone on the dance floor and Jake truly was her fiancé. For a brief moment if she closed her eyes, she could forget Miss Trufitt even existed and could give rein to her fantasies, and believe fairy stories did sometimes come true. All too soon, the dance ended and he escorted her back to their table.

Simon claimed her for the next dance — a lively quickstep, cheerfully telling her she was blooming and Jake was damned lucky. He made her laugh, teasing her in a brotherly way while she retaliated by asking how he was making out with Sandra.

'Well,' he whispered secretively in her ear, 'we wouldn't want to start any rumours, but we're getting along fine, though it's early days.'

'I'm delighted for you both. You two seemed to click right away. She's a very capable woman and will make an excellent doctor's wife.'

He grinned. 'You aren't match-making by any chance, are you? Sandra and I met several years ago,' he informed her. 'She stayed at our house when Mother took in a few visitors. That was when I was an innocent, shy, bashful youth and I daren't even speak to her.'

'Never!' Lexie chuckled. 'I don't believe you. You're having me on.'

'Believe you me, women terrify me,

but I've learned to conceal the fact.'

'What about the lovely Camilla?'

'What about her? You shouldn't believe all the gossip you hear, Lexie. There never was anything between us. She was amusing herself. Perhaps felt like slumming for a change. After all, I'm merely a humble doctor, certainly not for the likes of her. I knew that from the start. She's far too expensive for my taste, but it was amusing while it lasted.'

'I'm glad she didn't cause you any heartache.'

'Not a chance. I know a scheming minx when I meet one,' he said, swinging her round exuberantly. Lexie had the feeling of being watched, and glanced across to where Jake and Camilla were sitting on the edge of the dance floor. Jake scowled in her direction, and she suspected he was annoyed see her enjoying Simon's company. Well, it served him right, she thought gleefully.

★　★　★

Jake made up his mind he would have to tell Lexie the truth at the earliest suitable moment. He loved her, and it was driving him crazy watching her innocently mixing with the guests. The farce had gone on far too long, and he wanted to know where he stood. She had demonstrated an amazing capacity for loyalty despite Camilla's machinations, but he couldn't help noticing the way her eyes lit up with pleasure whenever she was with Simon Jackson. He didn't want her to get hurt. She didn't deserve to be hurt. She was an angel, just like her mother. Was Lexie eager to make her escape? Could he persuade her they could make wonderful music together once he got this deal with Joe wrapped up? He had intended waiting until after the New Year to discover whether she saw him only as the brother, or if there was a chance. Perhaps she thought he was too old. At times he managed to convince himself she was attracted to him, and on the rare occasions he took her in his arms she was warm and loving as a kitten. He loved the way her eyes altered with her moods, from ice-crystal cold to soft muted sea green with an almost fey quality.

Camilla nudged his arm. 'She's making a spectacle of herself again,' she sneered. 'Why do you allow it?'

'I beg your pardon?' he replied with a shake of the head. He'd forgotten all about Camilla sitting next to him.

'Your devoted fiancée, that's who I was talking about. Hadn't you noticed? You've been glaring in her direction for the last five minutes.'

'I was miles away thinking about the new project.'

'I was saying I'm leaving tomorrow for America. Pa's a bit miffed, but it can't be helped. Some friends have invited me to see the New Year in at their ranch.'

'Care for a last dance then?' He flashed her a brief smile. 'For old times' sake.'

They could relax for a few days before New Year, so Lexie spent as much of the time as she could out of the flat, and when not working either out walking or with her parents. Unfortunately they kept on about the forthcoming wedding arrangements. She had to steer them on to stories about their honeymoon trip, and the prospect of returning to Ravenstone to see the conversion. She knew she didn't sound excited as a newly engaged person should, but hoped her mother would think it was because she was working hard. Both of them looked so happy, and Lexie thought she had never seen her mother so vivacious. Now she knew what 'radiant as a bride' meant! It was wonderful what genuine love did, she thought wryly.

She only had to look at herself in the mirror to know what *unrequited* love did. She knew she was looking pale and had lost weight despite the magnificent concoctions the chef prepared for Christmas. She wondered if she would ever find anyone else to set her heart on fire the way Jake did. She couldn't understand why she should feel as she did when Jake gave her no encouragement. He hardly seemed to know she was there most of the time.

* * *

The New Year festivities were if anything more wild and exhausting. Lexie had seen nothing like it. For the most part she was swept along with the noise and lively repartee. She had hardly sat down all night, trying as she was to obliterate from her mind the thought of becoming a modern-day Cinderella. She knew when midnight struck what she had to do, and it brought a lump to her throat every time she thought about it.

*Ten, nine, eight,* the crowd counted. Jake's arms held her close as they were crushed on all sides by the happy revellers. She gazed up at him with sad, tear-filled eyes. It had been a marvellous time in many ways, but now was the moment of truth, and all that had happened would soon be just a memory. She had learned a lot during her stay at Thornton Grange and felt the experience would stand her in good stead. She would not have believed so much could happen over so short a period of time, but now she had to make a fresh start. She had no idea what she was going to do, except she had to get as far away as possible from Jake and Thornton Grange. Then maybe she could throw herself wholeheartedly into a new job and, in time, sort herself out emotionally.

'Why so sad, Lexie?' Jake was shouting to make himself heard over the noisy well-wishers. Pulling her onto a window seat a little apart from the crowd, he repeated, 'Lexie, what's wrong? Why are you upset?' Dabbing her tears away with his handkerchief, he looked puzzled as he tried to comfort her. He really did appear concerned, but she knew it wasn't genuine.

'Because it's all over,' she sobbed. 'All over.' It felt wrong to be so unhappy in such a lively, boisterous crowd. Somehow their merriment made her all the sadder because she couldn't feel part of it. 'Tomorrow is the start of a New Year. I hope I've fulfilled my part of the bargain to your satisfaction. I tried.'

Jake seemed to be having difficulty in accepting her resignation, as if he couldn't comprehend what she was saying. 'You can't leave now. I thought you liked working here. Please, Lexie, stay a little while longer.'

She shook her head, desperately trying to hold her composure. 'There's no reason to. I've heard of your plans for Alex and my mother to take over the running of Thornton Grange while you go on holiday. I also know Camilla's left, so there's no need for the charade to continue. You don't need me anymore. I'm sorry about Camilla; I really thought she was in love with you.' Twisting off the ring, she thrust it into his hand. 'Let me know what I owe you, but I can't face all this anymore.'

She ran from the room, almost bumping into Simon and Sandra standing near the doorway, arms round each other. It was not how she had intended the evening to end, but it was done now. Jake was free to do as he pleased. She thought she could be cool and unemotional as she handed him back his ring, but it hadn't been that easy. He had been at his most attentive all evening because Camilla wasn't present, and she had enjoyed his company even though it was insincere. Somehow she had wished and wished all could end happily, but she could not change the truth.

'Are you all right, Lexie?' she heard Simon call after her, but she was too upset to stop and ran blindly out of the hotel. Little flakes of snow drifted down and settled on the shrubbery, but she was oblivious to them, as she was oblivious to the cold and the watery crescent moon shining through a break in the clouds. It was a beautiful scene, but she was too preoccupied to notice. Slumping onto a garden seat, she broke down, sobbing her heart out. It was finally all over between them. She had made the decision, done what was necessary and let him off the hook.

Simon found her there. 'Whatever is the matter, Lexie? What's wrong?' he asked, draping his jacket round her shoulders. He pulled her into the shelter of his arms and rocked her gently. 'I thought something was amiss the other day when you went walkabout.'

'He doesn't love me,' she sobbed. 'It was all a mistake. I have to get away.'

'Hush now. Don't get upset.' Simon held her close, stroking her hair soothingly. 'Whatever it is can be sorted out.'

'I might have known I'd find you at the bottom of all this, Simon Jackson!'

Jake called. 'You're always around, acting the gallant protector, aren't you? You've wanted Lexie from the start, haven't you?'

'Don't be daft, Jake,' Simon said. 'She almost knocked me down when she came rushing out here. She wasn't wearing a coat and I could see how distressed she was. I came to see if I could help, that's all. I wasn't trying to come between you. Why would I do such a thing, for heaven's sake? You've only got to look at her to realise that she's — '

'I've seen the way the two of you behave while you think I'm not looking!' Jake growled. 'Well, may the best man win. Lexie will have to make her own choice.' With a disgusted look, he turned on his heel and stormed back inside.

'What on earth is going on?' Simon, looking totally bewildered, stared after him. 'What's got into Jake? I've never seen him like that. I know love does strange things to one, but . . . '

'It was all a charade.' Lexie tried to get a hold of herself, not paying any attention to Jake's allegations. 'The engagement was a put-up job. He didn't want Camilla to think he was free and available, so I had to pretend to be his fiancée.'

Simon looked unconvinced. 'So what's the problem? Camilla left for the States.'

Lexie lowered her head. 'The problem is I love him, but he doesn't love me,' she said, snuffling miserably. 'He still loves her, that's the problem. I can't take it any longer. I have to get away and try to forget him.'

Simon shook his head. 'I think you're mistaken. In fact I'm certain you are. I've known Jake for a good few years, so I think I should be the better judge, don't you? I know he's not one to display his heart on his sleeve. He's rather a sensitive individual actually, a lot like me, and I have the distinct impression he's mad about you. I've been on the receiving end of many black looks recently for talking to you, so don't tell me now I'm matchmaking.'

Lexie smiled wanly. 'Believe me, Camilla dented his ego when she went off and left him earlier this year, but he still wants her back. He wanted to make her jealous, and he seems satisfied at having achieved it, so he doesn't need me now. I suppose Camilla wants him to go chasing after her and he's a bit annoyed by her games. You know what she's like.'

Simon remained unconvinced. 'Look, you can't stay out here. You'll catch your death of cold. Come back inside and let's get you a drink. You look as if you could do with one; you're as white as a sheet. This is no way to start the New Year, my girl. I prescribe a large brandy. Things will seem much better in daylight.'

'I'm sorry, Simon.' She dried her eyes. 'I'll be all right, but I can't face anyone again tonight. I'm sorry. I've spoilt your shirt. I'll go to my room by way of the fire escape. Thanks for everything.' Giving him a brave smile, she handed him back his jacket. 'Go and enjoy the rest of the festivities. Don't let me spoil your fun. Sandra will be missing you.'

# 11

Lexie made her way across the car park, shivering with the cold. The flakes were coming down faster now, covering the steps of the fire escape with a thin layer of virgin snow making them wet and slippery. She wished she could disappear — vanish into the night, but she knew that first of all she had to explain everything to her parents. It wasn't a task she relished, not tonight. First thing in the morning, though . . .

On entering the lounge, which was all in darkness, she closed and locked the patio door, then waited a moment until her eyes became accustomed to the gloom. Shaking droplets of water off her hair caused by the melted snow, she wasn't immediately aware of the other occupant of the room. As she was about to make her way to the fire to warm herself, Jake's voice stopped her in her tracks.

'Sent him packing have you?' He was standing with his back to the fire, a whisky glass in his hand.

Lexie felt quite calm now. The scene had helped put things into perspective, but the thought of another confrontation was unwelcome. 'I'm going to bed,' she said quietly but firmly. 'I'll leave first thing in the morning.' Jake would have to accept things couldn't go on as they were, so the sooner she left the better. It would probably break her heart, but better to do it now while she could still hold her head up. She had given it her best shot, but Camilla had won in the end, and he was welcome to her.

'But you agreed to stay until the flats are complete, and only the first one has progressed that far. You always keep your promises, you told me,' he said.

'Jake, it's no use. I can't take any more,' she cried, the hurt building up until it was unbearable. 'You don't need me, so why try to keep me here? Go after Camilla. That's what she wants. She's only playing hard to get. You love her, so there's no point in prolonging things.'

He gave a smothered oath. 'You belong here, Lexie. I've no intention of chasing after Camilla. I told you I can't stand the woman. I'm glad she's gone.' Having put down his glass carefully on the mantelpiece, he walked round the back of the sofa towards her.

'Jake, this has to end,' she said quietly, with a great deal more composure than she felt. 'In the morning I shall tell my parents everything, including how I came to get Bay View to near bankruptcy. Something I should have admitted weeks ago. Then, even if I have to scrub floors for the rest of my days, I'll repay you every penny you've paid out on our behalf. But I won't be put into such an invidious position any longer by you or anyone else.'

He rubbed the back of his head irritably. 'I'm sorry. You're right, of course. I had no right to ask you to do anything of the sort. You were getting the backwash from what I endured at the hands of my mother and Camilla. It's been a hell of a year.' He gave a great sigh. 'Come and sit down and let me get you a drink. This is no way to start the New Year.'

Lexie hesitated, then went to sit on the sofa. She accepted a martini and lemonade, and sipped it gingerly. He replenished his own drink and sat next to her, but she noticed he put his glass on the side table untouched.

'It started with the death of my mother last March when I flew out for the funeral. I hadn't seen Alex for such a long time, and I was absolutely appalled at the state he was in. Mother had worn him out — he was a pale shadow of his former self. Unfortunately I was in the middle of extensive renovation work here at the time so could only stay for a few days. To cut a long story short, Alex insisted he would be all right coping with the necessary clearing up, and then promised to come to England. While I was away, Camilla — my supposed fiancée — upped and left with a guest from the hotel, and I returned to find a 'Dear John' letter waiting for me.' He placed a hand on her arm.

'It was only my pride that was hurt, Lexie I promise you. I soon realised what a fool I'd been. She was another predatory woman like my mother, and I was well rid of her. After that, I began to think all women were alike, and I was determined I wasn't going to get involved that way ever again. Women were out of my life for good. Then I met you. I tried to like you for Alex's sake. He was overjoyed to find he had a daughter, but I never really got past your sensational eyes. Such intriguing, treacherous eyes, I thought. You weren't going to make a fool out of me like Camilla had! No way. Not at any price.

'When I saw your financial condition, I thought you were turning out to be like my mother — out for all you could get, and I was determined you weren't going to get away with it. But I had to do it without upsetting Alex. I took advantage of the situation you found yourself in and decided to take my problems out on you. I'm sorry, Lexie. I realise I've badly misjudged you. You certainly didn't deserve the treatment I've meted out.'

Lexie twirled the glass round in her hands, wondering what was coming next. He sounded contrite at least, which gave her hope.

Jake got up and went to stand for a moment, gazing at the fire with his hands propped against the mantelpiece, his back to Lexie. She stared at his broad shoulders and waited, hardly daring to breathe as her optimism rose.

He turned eventually, grim-faced, his voice low. 'Alex could easily have arranged the funding for the flat alterations, and by rights should have done, but I decided I wasn't having that. I wanted you to stay at at Thornton Grange.' He picked up his drink again. 'Oh, I've been so stupid! I wanted to find fault with you — only that didn't work either, did it? You coped with everything so magnificently; and to cap it all, I was in danger of losing you to Simon Jackson. I even thought up the scheme to have you here in my flat in the hope that it would put an end to your association with him.'

'I thought it was because you wanted to make Camilla jealous,' Lexie said quietly, her heart beating with suppressed excitement.

'I wanted her to be jealous all right, to show her I didn't care a fig about her,' he said, returning to sit beside her on the settee.

'But you haven't got over her, have you? You still love her, don't you?' she said flatly, and finished her drink with a gulp. She smiled wryly. 'That's why you're so angry, isn't it? Because she's gone again, but . . . '

'No, Lexie,' he shouted, taking her by the shoulders. 'I told you I never loved her. I despise her. She's vain, selfish, conniving and thoroughly spoilt — all the things you're not. You, my beloved Lexie, brought a new meaning to my life, only it took a little time for me to see it. I could have dealt with Camilla — no problem. No, my main concern was how to get you away from Simon. How could I compete with the dashing young doctor? He's every woman's dream, isn't he? Most of the female members of staff seem to idolise him, I gather, so I assumed you weren't immune.'

Her heart skipped a beat. Could she really believe what she was hearing? Did he truly mean he loved her? After believing him to be in love with Camilla for so long, she found it hard to accept, much as she wanted to. 'I honestly don't know what to think. You've used and deceived me. I've even been made to lie to my parents. It's all been too much. These last three months have made me doubt my own sanity.'

'I'm sorry. What can I do to put things right? Anything, sweetheart — just name it. I'll even eat humble pie and tell Alex what I've done, if you want.'

'You can start by being completely honest with me, Jake. Why were you being so friendly with Camilla if you say you don't love her anymore? You never looked as if you found her attentions unwelcome.'

He gave a hollow laugh. 'That's easy to explain. It's all to do with the business deal which Joe, Alex and I are putting together.'

'Why didn't you tell me more about this sooner? I thought you were only being friendly with Joe because of Camilla.'

'Oh no,' he said adamantly. 'Not at all. I was putting up with Camilla's antics because we need Joe's backing for this project. Without it, the deal falls through. It's too late to go elsewhere for the financial support we need; besides which, we trust him. I couldn't tell you about it before because it still isn't finalised. I learned the hard way to trust no one.'

'I can understand that I suppose,' she replied, 'but can you tell me now what the deal is about that made Camilla's alliance so important?'

'Do you remember the last time we went to Ravenstone, and we came back by a slightly different route?'

She nodded. 'I thought at first you'd got lost, but then when I saw the farmhouse I thought it was probably where you were born.'

'That was a good guess, but wrong I'm afraid. I went to inspect the site for the proposed new development we're planning — a hotel, motel, sports complex and chalet park.'

'Good heavens. Are you going to be masterminding all that?'

'Mostly it will be down to Alex. He's the engineer. It's taken some complicated negotiating, but with a bit of luck, next week should see everything wrapped up.'

'And that's why you want a flat at Bay View, so you can have somewhere to live while you oversee the work.'

'Hmm, yes, that's right. It seemed to make a lot of sense, since both Alex and I will need to be in the area on and off for a good deal of the time for the next year or two, if we pull it off.'

'I don't see where that leaves me,' she said with a sigh of resignation. 'If you've got Joe's backing . . . ?'

He shook his head. 'Until all the documents are signed, nothing can be taken for granted. There's still time for Joe to pull out. He hasn't signed on the dotted line. I thought maybe Camilla would somehow put her spoke in and persuade her father to sign only if I became involved with her again. She's the apple of his eye and as devious as they come.'

Lexie stiffened. 'I see. So you want me to carry on this farce for a few more days until you have Joe hooked, and then I can have my cards, is that it?' Her eyes flashed angrily, and she thumped her glass down on the coffee table. 'Well no deal. I won't be a party to it any longer. I've had enough — I'm leaving.'

'Lexie, please listen to me. I'm not explaining this very well. I'm trying my best to apologise and to tell you that I love you, but I realise it's Simon you really want. I shouldn't have come between you. I can see that now, and I'm sorry. I suppose you want to leave because of Sandra? It does rather look as if they may make a go of things, and it's all my fault. It's always been Simon, hasn't it? If I hadn't cooked up this phoney engagement, you two might have — '

'Whatever gave you that idea?' Lexie asked with surprise. She flopped against the cushions, quite taken aback.

'It's obvious,' he replied, shrugging his shoulders. 'You always look so happy and light-hearted in his company. He makes you laugh, which is something I don't seem able to do, and he's nearer your own age after all. Then of course you admitted it — that night when you were delirious, you told me you loved him.'

'I did nothing of the sort!'

'Oh but you did, Lexie. Honestly. You were rambling on a bit, but I heard you say very clearly you loved him over and over. You also said you never wanted to leave Thornton Grange, so I didn't know what to make of that except maybe you hoped to continue working here so as to be near him.'

Lexie gasped. 'Oh, Jake, you've got it all wrong. Simon is a good friend — a very valued friend. I'm delighted he and Sandra are together. I couldn't be happier for both of them. If you must know, it's you I love, and always has been. But I'm nothing like Camilla. I'm not smart or sophisticated.'

'I don't understand . . . You and he always seem so . . . Lexie, do you really mean it? As for comparing you with Camilla, there really is no contest. You have a wonderful simplicity which I find utterly adorable.'

As she flew into his arms sobbing with delight, the phone rang. Jake cursed, reached across and snatched the receiver. His tone was terse as she heard him say wearily he'd be right down. Pulling her back into his embrace, he hugged her lovingly.

'What rotten timing. I'm sorry, my love, but this happens every year without fail. Some of the guests get too enthusiastic and mayhem erupts. This year apparently they're throwing people into the swimming pool. I'm afraid I'll have to go down and try to sort it out.'

'Need any help?' she asked with a despairing sigh.

'You'd best go to bed. It may take some time — it usually does. But before I go, the first priority is to put this back where it belongs.' He fished in his pocket and produced the ring, which he proceeded to replace on her finger. Gently tipping her head up to look at him, he kissed the tip of her nose. 'I bought this ring especially for you, my beloved. I hoped to convince you in time that I was sincere, but things have got out of hand recently. I've been rather too preoccupied with this business deal to have time with you. I thought once the New Year festivities were over, we could start getting to know one another in a more relaxed atmosphere. I even hoped to persuade you to join me on holiday.'

'You do truly love me?' she asked incredulously, still having difficulty believing it was real.

He groaned and devoured her with kisses. 'I must get a manager in soon. It should be his job to deal with this.' Finally he broke away. 'I have to go, dammit. Sleep well, sweet Lexie. We'll talk some more in the morning, OK?'

★  ★  ★

The next morning Lexie woke early. She lay for a moment reflecting on what had occurred, held out her hand and gazed at the ring. It was hers for keeps. He loved her! Everything was going to be all right. She was going to be Mrs Jake Thornton. Oh what a wonderful, wonderful way to start the New Year!

She hadn't heard Jake return even though she had stayed awake for a long time. It must have been quite some shindig. She wondered what damage had been caused by the merrymakers and hoped nobody had got hurt. Thinking it advisable to let Jake sleep, she quietly dressed and went to look around the hotel. The staff were already making great strides at restoring order and she began helping too. Around mid-morning, Simon dropped in and she waved the ring triumphantly under his nose.

'I'm glad he's come to his senses,' he said with a chuckle. 'Heaven knows what sort of life he would have led with Camilla for a wife, besides which it makes it easier for me now I don't have to choose between you and Sandra.'

She laughed. 'You'll find her in the dining room, I believe.'

Lexie poured a cup of coffee and took it back to the flat. All was quiet as she made her way to Jake's bedroom. She tapped lightly on the door and entered. Cautiously she approached the bed, feeling vaguely shy. He had his back towards her so she didn't know if he was awake. 'Fancy some coffee?' she asked, putting it down on the bedside table.

'I'd rather have you,' he replied, rolling over to grab her, and pulling her down on to the bed. 'Now, where were we when we were so inconsiderately interrupted last night, or was it earlier this morning?'

She laughed nervously. The sight of his bare torso was quite breathtaking. She reached up and ran her fingers through his tousled hair. 'I believe you were telling me how much you love me.'

'Hmm. You wouldn't care to join me in here, would you? This may take some time.'

'I'd love to, but unfortunately it's chaos downstairs, and . . . '

Jake growled. 'I don't want to know. It was after four when I got to bed.' Turning her onto her back, he began inundating her with kisses; then he looked serious. 'Lexie, please don't take this the wrong way, but can you tell me why your birthday is the first of August? It's been bothering me, and I just don't like mysteries.'

She looked affronted, then smiled mischievously. 'So you doubt my authenticity, do you?'

'No ... of course I don't. Its just ... '

She laughed. 'All right, I'll tell you. I nearly didn't make it. I was a premature baby and spent the first few weeks in an incubator. So there.'

Jake looked shocked. 'I'm so glad you made it. So when will you marry me, my darling?'

'Soon.' She grinned, revelling in the smooth texture of his skin as she caressed his taut muscles. 'But there's so much to arrange. Dresses to buy, flowers, the church, the reception ... '

'You've teased me long enough, my little enchantress. I need you beside me always. How about we get a special licence. You don't really want a lot of fuss and paraphernalia, do you? How about a nice simple wedding followed by a lovely long honeymoon?'

Lexie felt she was in paradise.